BALCONY STORIES

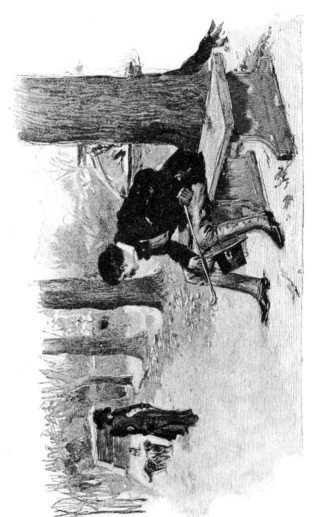

"WALKING AWAY WITH A SHRUG OF THE SHOULDERS."

BALCONY STORIES

BY

GRACE KING

AUTHOR OF "TALES OF A TIME AND PLACE"

THE GREGG PRESS / RIDGEWOOD, N. J.

First published in 1892 by The Century Co.
Republished in 1968 by
The Gregg Press Incorporated
171 East Ridgewood Avenue
Ridgewood, New Jersey, U.S.A.

Library of Congress Catalog Card Number: 68-23722

Printed in United States of America

AMERICANS IN FICTION

In the domain of literature the play may once have been the chief abstract and chronicle of the times, but during the nineteenth and twentieth centuries the novel has usurped the chief place in holding the mirror up to the homely face of society. On this account, if for no other, the Gregg Press series of reprints of American fiction merits the attention of all students of Americana and of librarians interested in building up adequate collections dealing with the social and literary history of the United States. Most of the three score and ten novels or volumes of short stories included in the series enjoyed considerable fame in their day but have been so long out of print as to be virtually unobtainable in the original editions.

Included in the list are works by writers not presently fashionable in critical circles—but nevertheless well known to literary historians—among them Joel Chandler Harris, Harriet Beecher Stowe, Thomas Bailey Aldrich, and William Gilmore Simms. A substantial element in the list consists of authors who are known especially for their graphic portrayal of a particular American setting, such as Gertrude Atherton (California), Arlo Bates (Boston), Alice Brown (New England), Edward Eggleston (Indiana), Mary Wilkins Freeman (New England), Henry B. Fuller (Chicago), Richard M. Johnston (Georgia), James Lane Allen (Kentucky), Mary N. Murfree (Tennessee), and Thomas Nelson Page (Virginia). There is even a novel by Frederic Remington, one of the most popular painters of the Western cowboy and Indian—and another, and impressive minor classic on the early mining region of Colorado, from the pen of Mary Hallock Foote. The professional student of American literature will rejoice in the opportunity afforded by the collection to extend his reading of fiction belonging to what is called the "local-color movement"—a major current in the development of the national belles-lettres.

Among the titles in the series are also a number of famous historical novels. Silas Weir Mitchell's *Hugh Wynne* is one of the very best fictional treatments of the American Revolution. John Esten Cooke is the foremost Southern writer of his day who dealt with the Civil War. The two books by Thomas Dixon are among the most famous novels on the Reconstruction Era, with sensational disclosures of the original Ku Klux Klan in action. They supplied the grist for the first great movie "spectacular"—*The Birth of a Nation* (1915).

Paul Leicester Ford's *The Honorable Peter Stirling* is justly ranked among the top American novels which portray American politics in action—a subject illuminated by other novelists in the Gregg list—A. H. Lewis, Frances H. Burnett, and Alice Brown, for example. Economic problems are forcefully put before the reader in works by Aldrich, Mrs. Freeman, and John Hay, whose novels illustrate the ominous concern over the early battles between labor and capital. From the sweatshops of Eastern cities in which newly arrived immigrants toiled for pittances, to the Western mining camps where the laborers packed revolvers, the working class of the times enters into various other stories in the Gregg list. The capitalist class, also, comes in for attention, with an account of a struggle for the ownership of a railroad in Samuel Merwin's *The Short-Line War* and with the devastating documentation of the foibles of the newly rich and their wives in the narratives of David Graham Phillips. It was Phillips whose annoying talent for the exposure of abuses led Theodore Roosevelt to put the term "muck-raker" into currency.

While it is apparent that local-color stories, the historical novel, and the economic novel have all been borne in mind in choosing the titles for this important series of reprints, it is evident that careful consideration has also been given to treatments of various minority elements in the American population. The Negro, especially, but also the Indian, the half-breed, Creoles, Cajuns—and even the West Coast Japanese—appear as characters in various of these novels or volumes of short stories and sketches. Joel Chandler Harris's *Free Joe* will open the eyes of readers who know that author solely as the creator of humorous old Uncle Remus. And there is a revelatory volume of dialect tales, written by a Negro author, *The Conjure Woman* by Charles W. Chesnutt.

In literary conventions and the dominating attitudes toward life, the works in the Gregg series range from the adventurous romance illustrated so well by Mayne Reid or the polite urbanity of Owen Wister to the mordant irony of Kate Chopin and the grimmer realism of Joseph Kirkland's own experiences on bloody Civil War battlefields or the depressing display of New York farm life by Harold Frederic. In short, the series admirably illustrates the general qualities of the fiction produced in the United States during the era covered, just as it generously mirrors the geographical regions, the people, and the problems of the times.

PROFESSOR CLARENCE GOHDES
Duke University
December, 1967 *Durham, North Carolina*

GRACE KING

Grace King (1852-1932) was born in New Orleans. She was educated in that city, and began her career by contributing to periodicals. When in 1886-1888, her *Creole Sketches* were published in the *New Princeton Review,* her reputation as an artist was established. Her subject matter was the rich and complex culture of New Orleans and the surrounding plantations, where Anglo-American, Negro, and French intermingled. Like George Washington Cable, Miss King brought into the literature of the South a new romantic regional element — the Louisiana Creole. *Balcony Stories* consists of fourteen short stories, "Experiences, reminiscences, episodes, picked up as only women know how to pick them up . . . and told as only women know how to relate them . . ." Each one is an exquisitely traced, intensely feminine sketch of the important events — that is to say, feelings — in the life of a woman. Her characters come from every level of New Orleans society; from "little Mammy" the nurse, with her instinctive knowledge of the mysteries of life and death, to the gorgeous daughters of the plantation nobility. There is a strong element of the pathetic in all of her characters — Mademoiselle Pupasse, whose "face resembled nothing so much as a little yellow apple shriveling from decay," "La Grande Demoiselle," once the most sought-after heiress in New Orleans, now reduced by the War to a figure of ridicule and misery. The picture of New Orleans plantation life which Miss King presents is so luxuriously tropical, so rich, leisured, and extravagantly pompous and colorful, that the author has to remind us that such a society really did in fact exist. *Balcony Stories* is not a novel of social criticism, although there is mention of conflict between classes and races — in one of her best stories, *The Little Convent Girl,* a child drowns herself in the Mississippi when she learns that her mother is colored. This tale is told so tactfully and objectively, however, that the author's personal feelings about miscegnation could never be divined from it. There are no didactic attacks on slavery as an institution, nor is there the patriotic fervor of William Gilmore Simms or John Esten Cooke. There is no overt indictment of the Yankees and their destruction of the old ways of life which she loved, for Miss King's aim is to create a work of art; stories which will entertain, and capture the subtle aura and fragrance of an exotic society which almost completely disappeared a hundred years ago.

PRINCIPAL WORKS: *Tales of Time and Place* (1888); *Earthlings* (1889); *Chevalier Alain de Triton* (1889); *Jean Baptiste Lemoine, Founder of New Orleans* (1892); *Balcony Stories* (1893); *New Orleans: The Place and the People* (1896); *De Soto and His Men in the Land of Florida* (1898); *History of Louisiana, Stories from History of Louisiana* (1916); *Pleasant Ways of St. Médard* (1916); *Creole Families of New Orleans* (1921); *Madame Girard, an Old French Teacher of New Orleans* (1922); *La Dame de Sainte Hermine* (1924).

F. C. S.

CONTENTS

LIST OF ILLUSTRATIONS

BALCONY STORIES

THE BALCONY

THERE is much of life passed on the balcony in a country where the summer
unrolls in six moon-lengths, and where the
nights have to come with a double endow-
ment of vastness and splendor to compensate
for the tedious, sun-parched days.

And in that country the women love to sit
and talk together of summer nights, on balconies, in their vague, loose, white garments,—
men are not balcony sitters,—with their sleeping children within easy hearing, the stars
breaking the cool darkness, or the moon
making a show of light—oh, such a discreet
show of light!—through the vines. And the
children inside, waking to go from one sleep

into another, hear the low, soft mother-voices
on the balcony, talking about this person and
that, old times, old friends, old experiences;
and it seems to them, hovering a moment in
wakefulness, that there is no end of the world
or time, or of the mother-knowledge; but, il-
limitable as it is, the mother-voices and the
mother-love and protection fill it all,—with
their mother's hand in theirs, children are not
afraid even of God,—and they drift into slum-
ber again, their little dreams taking all kinds
of pretty reflections from the great unknown
horizon outside, as their fragile soap-bubbles
take on reflections from the sun and clouds.

Experiences, reminiscences, episodes, picked
up as only women know how to pick them up
from other women's lives,—or other women's
destinies, as they prefer to call them,—and told
as only women know how to relate them;
what God has done or is doing with some
other woman whom they have known—that
is what interests women once embarked on
their own lives,—the embarkation takes place

at marriage, or after the marriageable time,—
or, rather, that is what interests the women
who sit of summer nights on balconies. For
in those long-moon countries life is open and
accessible, and romances seem to be furnished
real and gratis, in order to save, in a languor-
breeding climate, the ennui of reading and
writing books. Each woman has a different
way of picking up and relating her stories, as
each one selects different pieces, and has a
personal way of playing them on the piano.

Each story *is* different, or appears so to her;
each has some unique and peculiar pathos in
it. And so she dramatizes and inflects it, trying to make the point visible to her apparent
also to her hearers. Sometimes the pathos
and interest to the hearers lie only in this—
that the relater has observed it, and gathered
it, and finds it worth telling. For do we not
gather what we have not, and is not our own
lacking our one motive? It may be so, for it
often appears so.

And if a child inside be wakeful and preco-

cious, it is not dreams alone that take on reflections from the balcony outside: through
the half-open shutters the still, quiet eyes look
across the dim forms on the balcony to the star-
spangled or the moon-brightened heavens beyond; while memory makes stores for the
future, and germs are sown, out of which the
slow, clambering vine of thought issues, one
day, to decorate or hide, as it may be, the
structures or ruins of life.

A DRAMA OF THREE

A DRAMA OF THREE

IT was a regular dramatic performance
every first of the month in the little cottage of the old General and Madame B——.

It began with the waking up of the General
by his wife, standing at the bedside with a cup
of black coffee.

"Hé! Ah! Oh, Honorine! Yes; the first
of the month, and affairs—affairs to be transacted."

On those mornings when affairs were to be
transacted there was not much leisure for the
household; and it was Honorine who consti-
tuted the household. Not the old dressing-
gown and slippers, the old, old trousers, and
the antediluvian neck-foulard of other days!
Far from it. It was a case of warm water
(with even a fling of cologne in it), of the
trimming of beard and mustache by Honorine,
and the black broadcloth suit, and the brown
satin stock, and that *je ne sais quoi de dégagé*

which no one could possess or assume like the old General. Whether he possessed or assumed it is an uncertainty which hung over the fine manners of all the gentlemen of his day, who were kept through their youth in Paris to cultivate *bon ton* and an education.

It was also something of a gala-day for Madame la Générale too, as it must be a gala-day for all old wives to see their husbands pranked in the manners and graces that had conquered their maidenhood, and exhaling once more that ambrosial fragrance which once so well incensed their compelling presence.

Ah, to the end a woman loves to celebrate her conquest! It is the last touch of misfortune with her to lose in the old, the ugly, and the commonplace her youthful lord and master. If one could look under the gray hairs and wrinkles with which time thatches old women, one would be surprised to see the flutterings, the quiverings, the thrills, the emotions, the coals of the heart-fires which death alone extinguishes, when he commands the tenant to vacate.

Honorine's hands chilled with the ice of sixteen as she approached scissors to the

white mustache and beard. When her finger-tips brushed those lips, still well formed
and roseate, she felt it, strange to say, on her
lips. When she asperged the warm water
with cologne,—it was her secret delight and
greatest effort of economy to buy this cologne,—she always had one little moment of
what she called faintness—that faintness
which had veiled her eyes, and chained her
hands, and stilled her throbbing bosom, when
as a bride she came from the church with him.
It was then she noticed the faint fragrance of
the cologne bath. Her lips would open as
they did then, and she would stand for a moment and think thoughts to which, it must
be confessed, she looked forward from month
to month. What a man he had been! In
truth he belonged to a period that would accept nothing less from Nature than physical
beauty; and Nature is ever subservient to
the period. If it is to-day all small men,
and to-morrow gnomes and dwarfs, we may
know that the period is demanding them from
Nature.

When the General had completed—let it
be called no less than the ceremony of—
his toilet, he took his chocolate and his

pain de Paris.   Honorine could not imagine
him breakfasting on anything but *pain de
Paris*.   Then he sat himself in his large arm-
chair before his escritoire, and began trans-
acting his affairs with the usual—

"But where is that idiot, that dolt, that
sluggard, that snail, with my mail?"

Honorine, busy in the breakfast-room:

"In a moment, husband.   In a moment."

"But he should be here now.   It is the
first of the month, it is nine o'clock, I am
ready; he should be here."

"It is not yet nine o'clock, husband."

"Not yet nine!   Not yet nine!   Am I
not up?   Am I not dressed?   Have I not
breakfasted before nine?"

"That is so, husband.   That is so."

Honorine's voice, prompt in cheerful ac-
quiescence, came from the next room, where
she was washing his cup, saucer, and spoon.

"It is getting worse and worse every day.
I tell you, Honorine, Pompey must be dis-
charged.   He is worthless.   He is trifling.
Discharge him!   Discharge him!   Do not
have him about!   Chase him out of the
yard!   Chase him as soon as he makes his
appearance!   Do you hear, Honorine?"

"WHERE IS THAT IDIOT, THAT DOLT, THAT SLUGGARD, THAT SNAIL, WITH MY MAIL?"

"You must have a little patience, husband."

It was perhaps the only reproach one could make to Madame Honorine, that she never learned by experience.

"Patience! Patience! Patience is the invention of dullards and sluggards. In a well-regulated world there should be no need of such a thing as patience. Patience should be punished as a crime, or at least as a breach of the peace. Wherever patience is found police investigation should be made as for smallpox. Patience! Patience! I never heard the word—I assure you, I never heard the word in Paris. What do you think would be said there to the messenger who craved patience of you? Oh, they know too well in Paris—a rataplan from the walking-stick on his back, that would be the answer; and a, 'My good fellow, we are not hiring professors of patience, but legs.'"

"But, husband, you must remember we do not hire Pompey. He only does it to oblige us, out of his kindness."

"Oblige us! Oblige me! Kindness! A negro oblige me! Kind to me! That is it;

that is it. That is the way to talk under the
new régime. It is favor, and oblige, and education, and monsieur, and madame, now. What.
child's play to call this a country—a govern-
ment! I would not be surprised"—jumping
to his next position on this ever-recurring first
of the month theme—"I would not be surprised if Pompey has failed to find the letter
in the box. How do I know that the mail
has not been tampered with? From day to
day I expect to hear it. What is to prevent?
Who is to interpose? The honesty of the officials? Honesty of the officials—that is good!
What a farce—honesty of officials! That is
evidently what has happened. The thought
has not occurred to me in vain. Pompey has
gone. He has not found the letter, and—
well; that is the end."

But the General had still another theory to
account for the delay in the appearance of his
mail which he always posed abruptly after the
exhaustion of the arraignment of the post-
office.

"And why not Journel?" Journel was their
landlord, a fellow of means, but no extraction,
and a favorite aversion of the old gentleman's.
"Journel himself? You think he is above it,

hé? You think Journel would not do such a
thing? Ha! your simplicity, Honorine—your
simplicity is incredible. It is miraculous. I
tell you, I have known the Journels, from
father to son, for—yes, for seventy-five years.
Was not his grandfather the overseer on my
father's plantation? I was not five years old
when I began to know the Journels. And
this fellow, I know him better than he knows
himself. I know him as well as God knows
him. I have made up my mind. I have made
it up carefully that the first time that letter
fails on the first of the month I shall have
Journel arrested as a thief. I shall land him
in the penitentiary. What! You think I shall
submit to have my mail tampered with by a
Journel? Their contents appropriated? What!
You think there was no coincidence in Journel's offering me his post-office box just the
month—just the month, before those letters
began to arrive? You think he did not have
some inkling of them? Mark my words,
Honorine, he did—by some of his subterranean methods. And all these five years he
has been arranging his plans—that is all.
He was arranging theft, which no doubt has
been consummated to-day. Oh, I have re-

gretted it—I assure you I have regretted it, that I did not promptly reject his proposition, that, in fact, I ever had anything to do with the fellow."

It was almost invariably, so regularly do events run in this world,—it was almost invariably that the negro messenger made his appearance at this point. For five years the General had perhaps not been interrupted as many times, either above or below the last sentence. The mail, or rather the letter, was opened, and the usual amount—three ten-dollar bills—was carefully extracted and counted. And as if he scented the bills, even as the General said he did, within ten minutes after their delivery, Journel made his appearance to collect the rent.

It could only have been in Paris, among that old retired nobility, who counted their names back, as they expressed it, "au de çà du déluge," that could have been acquired the proper manner of treating a "roturier" landlord: to measure him with the eyes from head to foot; to hand the rent—the ten-dollar bill—with the tips of the fingers; to scorn a look at the humbly tendered receipt; to say: "The cistern needs repairing, the

roof leaks; I must warn you that unless such
notifications meet with more prompt attention
than in the past, you must look for another
tenant," etc., in the monotonous tone of su-
premacy, and in the French, not of Journel's
dictionary, nor of the dictionary of any such
as he, but in the French of Racine and Cor-
neille; in the French of the above suggested
circle, which inclosed the General's memory,
if it had not inclosed—as he never tired of
recounting—his star-like personality.

A sheet of paper always infolded the bank-
notes. It always bore, in fine but sexless
tracery, " From one who owes you much."

There, that was it, that sentence, which,
like a locomotive, bore the General and his
wife far on these firsts of the month to two
opposite points of the horizon, in fact, one
from the other—" From one who owes you
much."

The old gentleman would toss the paper
aside with the bill receipt. In the man to
whom the bright New Orleans itself almost
owed its brightness, it was a paltry act to
search and pick for a debtor. Friends had
betrayed and deserted him; relatives had forgotten him; merchants had failed with his

2

money; bank presidents had stooped to de-
ceive him; for he was an old man, and had
about run the gamut of human disappoint-
ments—a gamut that had begun with a C
major of trust, hope, happiness, and money.

His political party had thrown him aside.
Neither for ambassador, plenipotentiary, sen-
ator, congressman, not even for a clerkship,
could he be nominated by it. Certes!
"From one who owed him much." He had
fitted the cap to a new head, the first of
every month, for five years, and still the list
was not exhausted. Indeed, it would have
been hard for the General to look anywhere
and not see some one whose obligations to
him far exceeded this thirty dollars a month.
Could he avoid being happy with such eyes?

But poor Madame Honorine! She who
always gathered up the receipts, and the
"From one who owes you much"; who
could at an instant's warning produce the
particular ones for any month of the past
half-decade. She kept them filed, not only
in her armoire, but the scrawled papers
—skewered, as it were, somewhere else—
where women from time immemorial have
skewered such unsigned papers. She was

not original in her thoughts—no more, for
the matter of that, than the General was.
Tapped at any time on the first of the month,
when she would pause in her drudgery to
reimpale her heart by a sight of the written characters on the scrap of paper, her
thoughts would have been found flowing
thus, "One can give everything, and yet
be sure of nothing."

When Madame Honorine said "everything," she did not, as women in such cases
often do, exaggerate. When she married
the General, she in reality gave the youth
of sixteen, the beauty (ah, do not trust the
denial of those wrinkles, the thin hair, the
faded eyes!) of an angel, the dot of an
heiress. Alas! It was too little at the
time. Had she in her own person united all
the youth, all the beauty, all the wealth,
sprinkled parsimoniously so far and wide
over all the women in this land, would she
at that time have done aught else with this
than immolate it on the burning pyre of the
General's affection? "And yet be sure of
nothing."

It is not necessary, perhaps, to explain that
last clause. It is very little consolation for

wives that their husbands have forgotten,
when some one else remembers.   Some one
else!   Ah! there could be so many some
one elses in the General's life, for in truth
he had been irresistible to excess.   But this
was one particular some one else who had
been faithful for five years.   Which one?

When Madame Honorine solves that enigma she has made up her mind how to act.

As for Journel, it amused him more and
more.   He would go away from the little
cottage rubbing his hands with pleasure (he
never saw Madame Honorine, by the way,
only the General).   He would have given
far more than thirty dollars a month for this
drama; for he was not only rich, but a great
farceur.

LA GRANDE DEMOISELLE

LA GRANDE DEMOISELLE

THAT was what she was called by everybody as soon as she was seen or described. Her name, besides baptismal titles, was Idalie Sainte Foy Mortemart des Islets. When she came into society, in the brilliant little world of New Orleans, it was the event of the season, and after she came in, whatever she did became also events. Whether she went, or did not go; what she said, or did not say; what she wore, and did not wear—all these became important matters of discussion, quoted as much or more than what the president said, or the governor thought. And in those days, the days of '59, New Orleans was not, as it is now, a one-heiress place, but it may be said that one could find heiresses then as one finds type-writing girls now.

Mademoiselle Idalie received her birth, and what education she had, on her parents' plantation, the famed old Reine Sainte Foy place, and it is no secret that, like the ancient kings of France, her birth exceeded her education.

It was a plantation, the Reine Sainte Foy, the richness and luxury of which are really well described in those perfervid pictures of tropical life, at one time the passion of philanthropic imaginations, excited and exciting over the horrors of slavery. Although these pictures were then often accused of being purposely exaggerated, they seem now to fall short of, instead of surpassing, the truth. Stately walls, acres of roses, miles of oranges, unmeasured fields of cane, colossal sugar-house — they were all there, and all the rest of it, with the slaves, slaves, slaves everywhere, whole villages of negro cabins. And there were also, most noticeable to the natural, as well as to the visionary, eye—there were the ease, idleness, extravagance, self-indulgence, pomp, pride, arrogance, in short the whole enumeration, the moral *sine qua non*, as some people considered it, of the wealthy slaveholder of aristocratic descent and tastes.

What Mademoiselle Idalie cared to learn she studied, what she did not she ignored;

and she followed the same simple rule untrammeled in her eating, drinking, dressing, and
comportment generally; and whatever discipline may have been exercised on the place,
either in fact or fiction, most assuredly none
of it, even so much as in a threat, ever at-
tainted her sacred person. When she was
just turned sixteen, Mademoiselle Idalie made
up her mind to go into society. Whether she
was beautiful or not, it is hard to say. It is
almost impossible to appreciate properly the
beauty of the rich, the very rich. The unfet-
tered development, the limitless choice of ac-
cessories, the confidence, the self-esteem, the
sureness of expression, the simplicity of purpose, the ease of execution—all these produce
a certain effect of beauty behind which one
really cannot get to measure length of nose,
or brilliancy of eye. This much can be said:
there was nothing in her that positively con-
tradicted any assumption of beauty on her
part, or credit of it on the part of others. She
was very tall and very thin with small head,
long neck, black eyes, and abundant straight
black hair,—for which her hair-dresser de-
served more praise than she,—good teeth, of
course, and a mouth that, even in prayer,

talked nothing but commands; that is about
all she had *en fait d'ornements*, as the mo-
distes say.   It may be added that she walked
as if the Reine Sainte Foy plantation extended
over the whole earth, and the soil of it were
too vile for her tread.   Of course she did not
buy her toilets in New Orleans.   Everything
was ordered from Paris, and came as regularly through the custom-house as the modes
and robes to the milliners.   She was furnished
by a certain house there, just as one of a royal
family would be at the present day.   As this
had lasted from her layette up to her sixteenth
year, it may be imagined what took place
when she determined to make her début.
Then it was literally, not metaphorically, *carte
blanche*, at least so it got to the ears of society.
She took a sheet of note-paper, wrote the date
at the top, added, "I make my début in No-
vember," signed her name at the extreme end
of the sheet, addressed it to her dressmaker
in Paris, and sent it.

It was said that in her dresses the very
handsomest silks were used for linings, and
that real lace was used where others put imitation,—around the bottoms of the skirts, for
instance,—and silk ribbons of the best qual-

ity served the purposes of ordinary tapes;
and sometimes the buttons were of real gold
and silver, sometimes set with precious stones.
Not that she ordered these particulars, but
the dressmakers, when given *carte blanche* by
those who do not condescend to details, so
soon exhaust the outside limits of garments
that perforce they take to plastering them inside with gold, so to speak, and, when the
bill goes in, they depend upon the furnishings
to carry out a certain amount of the contract
in justifying the price. And it was said that
these costly dresses, after being worn once or
twice, were cast aside, thrown upon the floor,
given to the negroes — anything to get them
out of sight. Not an inch of the real lace,
not one of the jeweled buttons, not a scrap
of ribbon, was ripped off to save. And it was
said that if she wanted to romp with her dogs
in all her finery, she did it; she was known
to have ridden horseback, one moonlight
night, all around the plantation in a white
silk dinner-dress flounced with Alençon. And
at night, when she came from the balls, tired,
tired to death as only balls can render one,
she would throw herself down upon her bed
in her tulle skirts,— on top, or not, of the

exquisite flowers, she did not care,— and
make her maid undress her in that position;
often having her bodices cut off her, because
she was too tired to turn over and have them
unlaced.

That she was admired, raved about, loved
even, goes without saying.   After the first
month she held the refusal of half the beaux
of New Orleans.   Men did absurd, undigni-
fied, preposterous things for her; and she?
Love?   Marry?   The idea never occurred to
her.   She treated the most exquisite of her
pretenders no better than she treated her
Paris gowns, for the matter of that.   She
could not even bring herself to listen to a
proposal patiently; whistling to her dogs, in
the middle of the most ardent protestations,
or jumping up and walking away with a shrug
of the shoulders, and a " Bah !"

Well!   Every one knows what happened
after '59.   There is no need to repeat.   The
history of one is the history of all.   But there
was this difference — for there is every shade
of difference in misfortune, as there is every
shade of resemblance in happiness.   Mortemart des Islets went off to fight.   That was
natural; his family had been doing that, he

thought, or said, ever since Charlemagne.
Just as naturally he was killed in the first
engagement. They, his family, were always
among the first killed; so much so that it
began to be considered assassination to fight
a duel with any of them. All that was in the
ordinary course of events. One difference in
their misfortunes lay in that after the city
was captured, their plantation, so near, con-
venient, and rich in all kinds of provisions,
was selected to receive a contingent of troops
—a colored company. If it had been a colored company raised in Louisiana it might
have been different; and these negroes mixed
with the negroes in the neighborhood,—and
negroes are no better than whites, for the
proportion of good and bad among them,—
and the officers were always off duty when
they should have been on, and on when they
should have been off.

One night the dwelling caught fire. There
was an immediate rush to save the ladies
Oh, there was no hesitation about that! They
were seized in their beds, and carried out in
the very arms of their enemies; carried away
off to the sugar-house, and deposited there.
No danger of their doing anything but keep

very quiet and still in their *chemises de nuit*, and their one sheet apiece, which was about all that was saved from the conflagration— that is, for them. But it must be remembered that this is all hearsay. When one has not been present, one knows nothing of one's own knowledge; one can only repeat. It has been repeated, however, that although the house was burned to the ground, and everything in it destroyed, wherever, for a year afterward, a man of that company or of that neighborhood was found, there could have been found also, without search-warrant, property that had belonged to the Des Islets. That is the story; and it is believed or not, exactly according to prejudice.

How the ladies ever got out of the sugar-house, history does not relate; nor what they did. It was not a time for sociability, either personal or epistolary. At one offensive word your letter, and you, very likely, examined; and Ship Island for a hotel, with soldiers for hostesses! Madame Des Islets died very soon after the accident—of rage, they say; and that was about all the public knew.

Indeed, at that time the society of New Orleans had other things to think about than the fate of the Des Islets. As for *la grande demoiselle*, she had prepared for her own oblivion in the hearts of her female friends. And the gentlemen,—her *preux chevaliers*,—they were burning with other passions than those which had driven them to her knees, encountering a little more serious response than "bahs" and shrugs. And, after all, a woman seems the quickest thing forgotten when once the important affairs of life come to men for consideration.

It might have been ten years according to some calculations, or ten eternities,—the heart and the almanac never agree about time,—but one morning old Champigny (they used to call him Champignon) was walking along his levee front, calculating how soon the water would come over, and drown him out, as the Louisianians say. It was before a seven-o'clock breakfast, cold, wet, rainy, and discouraging. The road was knee-deep in mud, and so broken up with hauling, that it was like walking upon waves to get over it. A shower poured down. Old Champigny was hurrying in when he saw a figure approaching. He had to stop to look at it, for it was worth while. The head was hidden by a green barege veil, which the showers had plentifully besprinkled with dew; a tall, thin figure. Figure! No; not even could it be called a figure: straight up and down, like a finger or a post; high-shouldered, and a step—a step like a plow-man's. No umbrella; no—nothing more, in fact. It does not sound so peculiar as when first related—something must be forgotten. The feet — oh, yes, the feet — they were like waffle-irons, or frying-pans, or anything of that shape.

Old Champigny did not care for women — he never had; they simply did not exist for him in the order of nature. He had been married once, it is true, about a half century before; but that was not reckoned against the existence of his prejudice, because he was *célibataire* to his finger-tips, as any one could see a mile away. But that woman *intrigué'd* him.

He had no servant to inquire from. He performed all of his own domestic work in the wretched little cabin that replaced his old home. For Champigny also belonged to the great majority of the *nouveaux pauvres*. He went out into the rice-field, where were

one or two hands that worked on shares with
him, and he asked them.   They knew immediately; there is nothing connected with the
parish that a field-hand does not know at
once.   She was the teacher of the colored

CHAMPIGNY.

public school some three or four miles away.
"Ah," thought Champigny, "some Northern
lady on a mission."   He watched to see her
return in the evening, which she did, of
course; in a blinding rain.   Imagine the

3

green barege veil then; for it remained always down over her face.

Old Champigny could not get over it that
he had never seen her before. But he must
have seen her, and, with his abstraction and
old age, not have noticed her, for he found
out from the negroes that she had been
teaching four or five years there. And he
found out also—how, is not important—that
she was Idalie Sainte Foy Mortemart des
Islets. *La grande demoiselle!* He had
never known her in the old days, owing to
his uncomplimentary attitude toward women,
but he knew of her, of course, and of her
family. It should have been said that his
plantation was about fifty miles higher up
the river, and on the opposite bank to Reine
Sainte Foy. It seemed terrible. The old
gentleman had had reverses of his own,
which would bear the telling, but nothing
was more shocking to him than this—that
Idalie Sainte Foy Mortemart des Islets
should be teaching a public colored school
for—it makes one blush to name it—seven
dollars and a half a month. For seven dollars and a half a month to teach a set of—
well! He found out where she lived, a little

cabin — not so much worse than his own, for
that matter — in the corner of a field; no
companion, no servant, nothing but food and
shelter. Her clothes have been described.

Only the good God himself knows what
passed in Champigny's mind on the subject.
We know only the results. He went and
married *la grande demoiselle*. How? Only
the good God knows that too. Every first
of the month, when he goes to the city to
buy provisions, he takes her with him — in
fact, he takes her everywhere with him.

Passengers on the railroad know them
well, and they always have a chance to see
her face. When she passes her old plantation *la grande demoiselle* always lifts her veil
for one instant—the inevitable green barege
veil. What a face! Thin, long, sallow, petrified! And the neck! If she would only tie
something around the neck! And her plain,
coarse cottonade gown! The negro women
about her were better dressed than she.

Poor old Champignon! It was not an act
of charity to himself, no doubt cross and dis-
agreeable, besides being ugly. And as for
love, gratitude!

MIMI'S MARRIAGE

MIMI'S MARRIAGE

THIS is how she told about it, sitting in her little room,—her bridal chamber,— not larger, really not larger than sufficed for the bed there, the armoire here, the bureau opposite, and the washstand behind the door, the corners all touching. But a nice set of furniture, quite *comme il faut*,—handsome, in fact,—as a bride of good family should have. And she was dressed very prettily, too, in her long white *negligée*, with plenty of lace and ruffles and blue ribbons,—such as only the Creole girls can make, and brides, alas! wear, —the pretty honeymoon costume that suggests, that suggests—well! to proceed. "The poor little cat!" as one could not help calling her, so *mignonne*, so blonde, with the pretty black eyes, and the rosebud of a mouth,— whenever she closed it,—a perfect kiss.

"But you know, Louise," she said, beginning quite seriously at the beginning, "papa

would never have consented, never, never—
poor papa! Indeed, I should never have
asked him; it would only have been one humiliation more for him, poor papa! So it
was well he was dead, if it was God's will for
it to be. Of course I had my dreams, like
everybody. I was so blonde, so blonde, and
so small; it seemed like a law I should marry
a *brun*, a tall, handsome *brun*, with a mustache and a fine barytone voice. That was
how I always arranged it, and—you will
laugh—but a large, large house, and numbers of servants, and a good cook, but a su-
perlatively good cuisine, and wine and all
that, and long, trailing silk dresses, and theater every night, and voyages to Europe, and
—well, everything God had to give, in fact.
You know, I get that from papa, wanting
everything God has to give! Poor papa!
It seemed to me I was to meet him at any
time, my handsome *brun*. I used to look for
him positively on my way to school, and back
home again, and whenever I would think of
him I would try and walk so prettily, and
look so pretty! *Mon Dieu!* I was not ten
years old yet! And afterward it was only for
that that I went into society. What should

girls go into society for otherwise but to meet
their *brun* or their blond? Do you think it
is amusing, to economize and economize, and
sew and sew, just to go to a party to dance?
No! I assure you, I went into society only
for that; and I do not believe what girls say
—they go into society only for that too.

" You know at school how we used to *tirer
la bonne aventure.*[1] Well, every time he was
not *brun, riche, avenant,* Jules, or Raoul, or
Guy, I simply would not accept it, but would
go on drawing until I obtained what I wanted.
As I tell you, I thought it was my destiny.
And when I would try with a flower to see if
he loved me,—*Il m'aime, un peu, beaucoup,
passionément, pas du tout,*—if it were *pas du
tout,* I would always throw the flower away,
and begin tearing off the leaves from another
one immediately. *Passionément* was what I
wanted, and I always got it in the end.

" But papa, poor papa, he never knew anything of that, of course. He would get furi-

[1] *La bonne aventure* is or was generally a very much battered
foolscap copy-book, which contained a list of all possible elements
of future (school-girl) happiness. Each item answered a question,
and had a number affixed to it. To draw one's fortune consisted in
asking question after question, and guessing a number, a companion
volunteering to read the answers. To avoid cheating, the books
were revised from time to time, and the numbers changed.

ous when any one would come to see me, and
sometimes, when he would take me in society,
if I danced with a 'nobody,'—as he called

no matter whom I danced with,—he would
come up and take me away with such an air
—such an air!   It would seem that papa
thought himself better than everybody in the

world. But it went worse and worse with
papa, not only in the affairs of the world, but
in health. Always thinner and thinner, always a cough; in fact, you know, I am a little feeble-chested myself, from papa. And
Clementine! Clementine with her children—
just think, Louise, eight! I thank God my
mama had only me, if papa's second wife had
to have so many. And so naughty! I assure
you, they were all devils; and no correction,
no punishment, no education—but you know
Clementine! I tell you, sometimes on account of those children I used to think myself in 'ell [making the Creole's attempt and
failure to pronounce the h], and Clementine
had no pride about them. If they had shoes,
well; if they had not shoes, well also.

"'But Clementine!' I would expostulate,
I would pray —

"'But do not be a fool, Mimi,' she would
say. 'Am I God? Can I do miracles? Or
must I humiliate your papa?'

"That was true. Poor papa! It would
have humiliated papa. When he had money
he gave; only it was a pity he had no money.
As for what he observed, he thought it was
Clementine's negligence. For, it is true,

Clementine had no order, no industry, in the best of fortune as in the worst. But to do her justice, it was not her fault this time, only she let him believe it, to save his pride; and Clementine, you know, has a genius for stories. I assure you, Louise, I was desperate. I prayed to God to help me, to advise me. I could not teach—I had no education; I could not go into a shop—that would be dishonoring papa—and *enfin*, I was too pretty. 'And proclaim to the world,' Clementine would cry, 'that your papa does not make money for his family.' That was true. The world is so malicious. You know, Louise, sometimes it seems to me the world is glad to hear that a man cannot support his family; it compliments those who can. As if papa had not intelligence, and honor, and honesty! But they do not count now as in old times, 'before the war.'

"And so, when I thought of that, I laughed and talked and played the thoughtless like Clementine, and made bills. We made bills —we had to—for everything; we could do that, you know, on our old name and family. But it is too long! I am sure it is too long and tiresome! What egotism on my part!

Come, we will take a glass of anisette, and talk of something else—your trip, your family. No? no? You are only asking me out of politeness! You are so *aimable*, so kind. Well, if you are not *ennuyée* — in fact, I want to tell you. It was too long to write, and I detest a pen. To me there is no instrument of torture like a pen.

"Well, the lady next door, she was an American, and common, very common, according to papa. In comparison to us she had no family whatever. Our little children were forbidden even to associate with her little children. I thought that was ridiculous— not that I am a democrat, but I thought it ridiculous. But the children cared; they were so disobedient and they were always next door, and they always had something nice to eat over there. I sometimes thought Clementine used to encourage their disobedience, just for the good things they got to eat over there. But papa was always making fun of them; you know what a sharp tongue he had. The gentleman was a clerk; and, according to papa, the only true gentlemen in the world had family and a profession. We did not dare allow ourselves to think it, but Clementine and I knew that they, in fact, were in more comfortable circumstances than we.

"The lady, who also had a great number of children, sent one day, with all the discretion and delicacy possible, and asked me if I would be so kind as to—guess what, Louise! But only guess! But you never could! Well, to darn some of her children's stockings for her. It was God who inspired her, I am sure, on account of my praying so much to him. You will be shocked, Louise, when I tell you. It sounds like a sin, but I was not in despair when papa died. It was a grief,— yes, it seized the heart, but it was not despair. Men ought not to be subjected to the humiliation of life; they are not like women, you know. We are made to stand things; they have their pride,—their *orgueil*, as we say in French,—and that is the point of honor with some men. And Clementine and I, we could not have concealed it much longer. In fact, the truth was crying out everywhere, in the children, in the house, in our own persons, in our faces. The darning did not provide a superfluity, I guarantee you!

"Poor papa! He caught cold. He was condemned from the first. And so all his

fine qualities died; for he had fine qualities —
they were too fine for this age, that was all.
Yes; it was a kindness of God to take him
before he found out.   If it was to be, it was
better.   Just so with Clementine as with me.
After the funeral — crack! everything went
to pieces.   We were at the four corners for
the necessaries of life, and the bills came in —
my dear, the bills that came in!   What memories! what memories!   Clementine and I exclaimed; there were some bills that we had
completely forgotten about.   The lady next
door sent her brother over when papa died.
He sat up all night, that night, and he as-
sisted us in all our arrangements.   And he
came in afterward, every evening.   If papa
had been there, there would have been a fine
scene over it; he would have had to take the
door, very likely.   But now there was no one
to make objections.   And so when, as I say,
we were at the four corners for the necessaries of life, he asked Clementine's permission
to ask me to marry him.

    "I give you my word, Louise, I had for-
gotten there was such a thing as marriage in
the world for me!   I had forgotten it as completely as the chronology of the Merovingian

dynasty, alas! with all the other school things
forgotten.   And I do not believe Clementine
remembered there was such a possibility in
the world for me.   *Mon Dieu!* when a girl
is poor she may have all the beauty in the
world — not that I had beauty, only a little
prettiness.   But you should have seen Clementine!   She screamed for joy when she told
me.   Oh, there was but one answer according to her, and according to everybody she
could consult, in her haste.   They all said it
was a dispensation of Providence in my favor.
He was young, he was strong; he did not
make a fortune, it was true, but he made a
good living.   And what an assistance to have
a man in the family!—an assistance for Clementine and the children.   But the principal
thing, after all, was, he wanted to marry me.
Nobody had ever wanted that before, my
dear!

"Quick, quick, it was all arranged.   All
my friends did something for me.   One made
my *peignoirs* for me, one this, one that—*ma
foi!* I did not recognize myself.   One made
all the toilet of the bureau, another of the
bed, and we all sewed on the wedding-dress
together.   And you should have seen Clem-

entine, going out in all her great mourning,
looking for a house, looking for a servant!
But the wedding was private on account of
poor papa. But you know, Loulou, I had
never time to think, except about Clementine
and the children, and when I thought of all
those poor little children, poor papa's children, I said 'Quick, quick,' like the rest.

"It was the next day, the morning after
the wedding, I had time to think. I was
sitting here, just as you see me now, in my
pretty new *negligée*. I had been looking at
all the pretty presents I have shown you, and
my trousseau, and my furniture,— it is not
bad, as you see,— my dress, my veil, my
ring, and — I do not know — I do not know
— but, all of a sudden, from everywhere
came the thought of my *brun*, my handsome
brun with the mustache, and the *bonne aventure, riche, avenant,* the Jules, Raoul, Guy,
and the flower leaves, and '*il m'aime, un peu,
beaucoup, pas du tout,*' *passionnément,* and
the way I expected to meet him walking
to and from school, walking as if I were
dancing the steps, and oh, my plans, my
plans, my plans,— silk dresses, theater, voyages to Europe,— and poor papa, so fine, so

4

tall, so aristocratic. I cannot tell you how
it all came; it seized my heart, and, *mon
Dieu!* I cried out, and I wept, I wept, I
wept. How I wept! It pains me here now
to remember it. Hours, hours it lasted, until I had no tears in my body, and I had to
weep without them, with sobs and moans.
But this, I have always observed, is the time
for reflection — after the tears are all out.
And I am sure God himself gave me my
thoughts. 'Poor little Mimi!' I thought,
'*fi donc!* You are going to make a fool of
yourself now when it is all over, because
why? It is God who manages the world,
and not you. You pray to God to help you
in your despair, and he has helped you. He
has sent you a good, kind husband who
adores you; who asks only to be a brother
to your sisters and brothers, and son to
Clementine; who has given you more than
you ever possessed in your life — but because
he did not come out of the *bonne aventure* —
and who gets a husband out of the *bonne
aventure?* — and would your *brun* have come
to you in your misfortune?' I am sure God
inspired those thoughts in me.

"I tell you, I rose from that bed — natu-

"I WEPT, I WEPT, I WEPT"

rally I had thrown myself upon it. Quick I washed my face, I brushed my hair, and, you see these bows of ribbons,— look, here are the marks of the tears, —I turned them. *Hé*, Loulou, it occurs to me, that if you examined the blue bows on a bride's *negligée*, you might always find tears on the other side; for do they not all have to marry whom God sends? and am I the only one who had dreams? It is the end of dreams, marriage; and that is the good thing about it. God lets us dream to keep us quiet, but he knows when to wake us up, I tell you. The blue bows knew! And now, you see, I prefer my husband to my *brun;* in fact, Loulou, I adore him, and I am furiously jealous about him. And he is so good to Clementine and the poor little children; and see his photograph — a blond, and not good-looking, and small!

"But poor papa! If he had been alive, I am sure he never would have agreed with God about my marriage."

THE MIRACLE CHAPEL

THE MIRACLE CHAPEL

EVERY heart has a miracle to pray for.
Every life holds that which only a miracle can cure. To prove that there have never
been, that there can never be, miracles does
not alter the matter. So long as there is
something hoped for,—that does not come in
the legitimate channel of possible events,—
so long as something does come not to be
hoped or expected in the legitimate channel
of possible events, just so long will the miracle be prayed for.

The rich and the prosperous, it would
seem, do not depend upon God so much, do
not need miracles, as the poor do. They do
not have to pray for the extra crust when
starvation hovers near; for the softening of
an obdurate landlord's heart; for strength in
temptation, light in darkness, salvation from
vice; for a friend in friendlessness; for that
miracle of miracles, an opportunity to strug-

gling ambition; for the ending of a dark
night, the breaking of day; and, oh! for God's
own miracle to the bedside-watchers — the
change for the better, when death is there
and the apothecary's skill too far, far away.
The poor, the miserable, the unhappy, they
can show their miracles by the score; that is
why God is called the poor man's friend. He
does not mind, so they say, going in the face
of logic and reason to relieve them; for often
the kind and charitable are sadly hampered
by the fetters of logic and reason, which
hold them, as it were, away from their own
benevolence.

But the rich have their miracles, no doubt,
even in that beautiful empyrean of moneyed
ease in which the poor place them. Their
money cannot buy all they enjoy, and God
knows how much of their sorrow it assuages.
As it is, one hears now and then of accidents
among them, conversions to better thoughts,
warding off of danger, rescue of life; and
heirs are sometimes born, and husbands provided, and fortunes saved, in such surprising
ways, that even the rich, feeling their limitations in spite of their money, must ascribe
it privately if not publicly to other potencies

than their own.   These cathedral *tours de
force*, however, do not, if the truth be told,
convince like the miracles of the obscure little chapel.

There is always a more and a most obscure
little miracle chapel, and as faith seems ever
to lead unhesitatingly to the latter one, there
is ever rising out of humility and obscurity,
as in response to a demand, some new shrine,
to replace the wear and tear and loss of other
shrines by prosperity.   For, alas! it is hard
even for a chapel to remain obscure and
humble in the face of prosperity and popularity.   And how to prevent such popularity
and prosperity?   As soon as the noise of a
real miracle in it gets abroad, every one is
for hurrying thither at once with their needs
and their prayers, their candles and their pic-
ayunes; and the little miracle chapel, perhaps despite itself, becomes with mushroom
growth a church, and the church a cathedral,
from whose resplendent altars the cheap,
humble ex-voto tablets, the modest begin-
nings of its ecclesiastical fortunes, are before
long banished to dimly lighted lateral shrines.

The miracle chapel in question lay at the
end of a very confusing but still intelligible

route.   It is not in truth a chapel at all, but
a consecrated chamber in a very small, very
lowly cottage, which stands, or one might
appropriately, if not with absolute novelty,
say which kneels, in the center of a large
garden, a garden primeval in rusticity and
size, its limits being defined by no lesser
boundaries than the four intersecting streets
outside, and its culture showing only the careless, shiftless culture of nature.   The streets
outside were miracles themselves in that, with
their liquid contents, they were streets and not
bayous.   However, they protected their island
chapel almost as well as a six-foot moat could
have done.   There was a small paved space on
the sidewalk that served to the pedestrian as
an indication of the spot in the tall, long, broad
fence where a gate might be sought.   It was
a small gate with a strong latch.   It required
a strong hand to open it.   At the sound of
the click it made, the little street ragamuffin,
who stood near, peeping through the fence,
looked up.   He had worked quite a hole between the boards with his fingers.   Such an
anxious expression passed over his face that
even a casual passer-by could not help reliev-
ing it by a question—any question:

"Is this the miracle chapel, little boy?"

"Yes, ma'am; yes." Then his expression changed to one of eagerness, yet hardly less anxious.

"Here. Take this —"

He did not hold out his hand, the coin had to seek it. At its touch he refused to take it.

"I ain't begging."

"What are you looking at so through the fence?" He was all sadness now.

"Just looking."

"Is there anything to see inside?"

He did not answer. The interrogation was repeated.

"I can't see nothing. I'm blind," putting his eyes again to the hole, first one, then the other.

"Come, won't you tell me how this came to be a miracle chapel?"

"Oh, ma'am,"— he turned his face from the fence, and clasped his hands in excitement,— "it was a poor widow woman who come here with her baby that was a-dying, and she prayed to the Virgin Mary, and the Virgin Mary made the baby live —"

He dropped his voice, the words falling slower and slower. As he raised his face, one

could see then that he was blind, and the
accident that had happened to him, in ford-
ing the street.   What sightless eyes !   What
a wet, muddy little skeleton !   Ten ?   No ;
hardly ten years of age.

"The widow woman she picked up her
baby, and she run down the walk here, and
out into the street screaming — she was so
glad,"— putting his eyes to the peep-hole
again,— "and the Virgin Mary come down
the walk after her, and come through the
gate, too ; and that was all she seed — the
widow woman."

"Did you know the widow woman ? "

He shook his head.

"How do you know it ? "

"That was what they told me.   And they
told me, the birds all begun to sing at once,
and the flowers all lighted up like the sun
was shining on them.   They seed her.   And
she come down the walk, and through the
gate," his voice lowering again to a whisper.

Ay, how the birds must have sung, and the
flowers shone, to the widowed mother as she
ran, nay, leaped, down that rose-hedged walk,
with her restored baby clasped to her bosom !

"*They* seed her," repeated the little fellow.

"And that is why you stand here—to see her, too?"

His shoulder turned uneasily in the clasp upon it.

"They seed her, and they ain't got no eyes."

"Have you no mother?"

"Ain't never had no mother." A thought struck him. "Would that count, ma'am? Would that count? The little baby that was dying — yes, ma'am, it had a mother; and it 's the mothers that come here constant with their children; I sometimes hear 'em dragging them in by the hand."

"How long have you been coming here?"

"Ever since the first time I heard it, ma'am."

Street ragamuffins do not cry: it would be better if they did so, when they are so young and so blind; it would be easier for the spectator, the auditor.

"They seed her — I might see her ef — ef I could see her once — ef — ef I could see anything once." His voice faltered; but he stiffened it instantly. "She might see me. She can't pass through this gate without seeing me; and—and — ef she seed me — and

I did n't even see her — oh, I 'm so tired of being blind!"

"Did you never go inside to pray?" How embarrassing such a question is, even to a child!

"No, ma'am. Does that count, too? The little baby did n't pray, the flowers did n't go inside, nor the birds. And they say the birds broke out singing all at once, and the flowers shined, like the sun was shining on 'em — like the sun was shining in 'em," he corrected himself. "The birds they can see, and the flowers they can't see, and they seed her." He shivered with the damp cold — and perhaps too with hunger.

"Where do you live?"

He would n't answer.

"What do you live on?"

He shook his head.

"Come with me." He could not resist the grasp on his shoulder, and the firm directing of his bare, muddy feet through the gate, up the walk, and into the chamber which the Virgin found that day. He was turned to the altar, and pressed down on his knees.

One should not look at the face of a blind child praying to the Virgin for sight. Only the Virgin herself should see that — and if she once saw that little boy! There were hearts, feet, hands, and eyes enough hanging around to warrant hope at least, if not faith; the effigies of the human aches and pains that had here found relief, if not surcease; feet and hands beholden to no physician for their exorcism of rheumatism; eyes and ears indebted to no oculist or aurist; and the hearts,— they are always in excess,— and, to the most skeptical, there is something sweetly comforting in the sight of so many cured hearts, with their thanks cut deep, as they should be, in the very marble thereof. Where the bed must have stood was the altar, rising by easy gradations, brave in ecclesiastical deckings, to the plaster figure of her whom those yearning hearts were seeing, whom those murmuring lips were addressing. Hearts must be all alike to her at such a distance, but the faces to the looker-on were so different. The eyes straining to look through all the experiences and troubles that their life has held to plead, as only eyes can plead, to one who can, if she will, perform their miracle for them. And the mouths,— the sensitive hu-

5

man mouths,— each one distorted by the
tragedy against which it was praying.

Their miracles! their miracles! what trifles
to divinity! Perhaps hardly more to humanity! How far a simple looker-on could supply them if so minded! Perhaps a liberal
exercise of love and charity by not more
than half a dozen well-to-do people could
answer every prayer in the room! But what
a miracle that would be, and how the Virgin's
heart would gladden thereat, and jubilate over
her restored heart-dying children, even as the
widowed mother did over her one dying babe!

And the little boy had stopped praying.
The futility of it — perhaps his own impo-
tence — had overcome him. He was crying,
and past the shame of showing it — crying
helplessly, hopelessly. Tears were rolling
out of his sightless eyes over his wordless
lips. He could not pray; he could only cry.
What better, after all, can any of us do? But
what a prayer to a woman — to even the
plaster figure of a woman! And the Virgin
did hear him; for she had him taken without
loss of a moment to the hospital, and how
easy she made it for the physician to remove
the disability! To her be the credit.

THE STORY OF A DAY

ANNE MARIE AND JEANNE MARIE

THE STORY OF A DAY

IT is really not much, the story; it is only the arrangement of it, as we would say of our dresses and our drawing-rooms.

It began with the dawn, of course; and the skiff for our voyage, silvered with dew, waiting in the mist for us, as if it had floated down in a cloud from heaven to the bayou. When repeated, this sounds like poor poetry; but that is the way one thinks at daydawn, when the dew is yet, as it were, upon our brains, and our ideas are still half dreams, and our waking hearts, alas! as innocent as waking babies playing with their toes.

Our oars waked the waters of the bayou, as motionless as a sleeping snake under its misty covert—to continue the poetical language or thought. The ripples ran frightened and shivering into the rooty thicknesses of the sedge-grown banks, startling the little birds bathing there into darting to the nearest, highest rush-top, where, without losing their hold on their swaying, balancing perches, they burst into all sorts of incoherent songs, in their excitement to divert attention from the near-hidden nests: bird mothers are so much like women mothers!

It soon became day enough for the mist to rise. The eyes that saw it ought to be able to speak to tell fittingly about it.

Not all at once, nor all together, but a thinning, a lifting, a breaking, a wearing away; a little withdrawing here, a little withdrawing there; and now a peep, and now a peep; a bride lifting her veil to her husband! Blue! White! Lilies! Blue lilies! White lilies! Blue and white lilies! And still blue and white lilies! And still! And still! Wherever the veil lifted, still and always the bride!

Not in clumps and bunches, not in spots and patches, not in banks, meadows, acres, but in—yes; for still it lifted beyond and beyond and beyond; the eye could not touch the limit of them, for the eye can touch only the limit of vision; and the lilies filled the whole sea-marsh, for that is the way spring comes to the sea-marshes.

The sedge-roots might have been unsightly along the water's edge, but there were morning-glories, all colors, all shades—oh, such morning-glories as we of the city never see! Our city morning-glories must dream of them, as we dream of angels. Only God could be so lavish! Dropping from the tall spear-heads to the water, into the water, under the water. And then, the reflection of them, in all their colors, blue, white, pink, purple, red, rose, violet!

To think of an obscure little Acadian bayou waking to flow the first thing in the morning not only through banks of new-blown morning-glories, but sown also to its depths with such reflections as must make it think itself a bayou in heaven, instead of in Paroisse St. Martin. Perhaps that is the reason the poor poets think themselves poets, on account of the beautiful things that are only reflected into their minds from what is above? Besides the reflections, there were alligators in the bayou, trying to slip away before we could see them, and watching us with their stupid, senile eyes, sometimes from under the thickest, prettiest flowery bowers; and turtles splashing into the water ahead of us; and

fish (silver-sided perch), looking like reflections themselves, floating through the flower
reflections, nibbling their breakfast.

Our bayou had been running through
swamp only a little more solid than itself; in
fact, there was no solidity but what came from
the roots of grasses. Now, the banks began
to get firmer, from real soil in them. We
could see cattle in the distance, up to their
necks in the lilies, their heads and sharp-
pointed horns coming up and going down in
the blue and white. Nothing makes cattle's
heads appear handsomer, with the sun just rising far, far away on the other side of them. The
sea-marsh cattle turned loose to pasture in the
lush spring beauty—turned loose in Elysium!

But the land was only partly land yet, and
the cattle still cattle to us. The rising sun
made revelations, as our bayou carried us
through a drove in their Elysium, or it might
have always been an Elysium to us. It was
not all pasturage, all enjoyment. The rising
and falling feeding head was entirely different,
as we could now see, from the rising and falling agonized head of the bogged—the buried
alive. It is well that the lilies grow taller
and thicker over the more treacherous places;

but, misery! misery! not much of the process
was concealed from us, for the cattle have to
come to the bayou for water. Such a splendid
black head that had just yielded breath! The
wide-spreading ebony horns thrown back
among the morning-glories, the mouth open
from the last sigh, the glassy eyes staring
straight at the beautiful blue sky above,
where a ghostly moon still lingered, the velvet
neck ridged with veins and muscles, the body
already buried in black ooze. And such a
pretty red-and-white-spotted heifer, lying on
her side, opening and shutting her eyes,
breathing softly in meek resignation to her
horrible calamity! And, again, another one
was plunging and battling in the act of real-
izing her doom: a fierce, furious, red cow,
glaring and bellowing at the soft, yielding
inexorable abysm under her, the bustards set-
tling afar off, and her own species browsing
securely just out of reach.

They understand that much, the sea-marsh
cattle, to keep out of reach of the dead com-
batant. In the delirium of anguish, relief
cannot be distinguished from attack, and
rescue of the victim has been proved to mean
goring of the rescuer.

The bayou turned from it at last, from our beautiful lily world about which our pleasant thoughts had ceased to flow even in bad poetry.

Our voyage was for information, which might be obtained at a certain habitation; if not there, at a second one, or surely at a third and most distant settlement.

The bayou narrowed into a canal, then widened into a bayou again, and the low, level swamp and prairie advanced into woodland and forest. Oak-trees began, our beautiful oak-trees! Great branches bent down almost to the water,— quite even with high water,— covered with forests of oak, parasites, lichens, and with vines that swept our heads as we passed under them, drooping now and then to trail in the water, a plaything for the fishes, and a landing-place for amphibious insects. The sun speckled the water with its flickering patterns, showering us with light and heat. We have no spring suns; our sun, even in December, is a summer one.

And so, with all its grace of curve and bend, and so — the description is longer than the voyage — we come to our first stopping-place. To the side, in front of the well-kept fertile fields, like a proud little showman, stood the little house. Its pointed shingle roof covered it like the top of a chafing-dish, reaching down to the windows, which peeped out from under it like little eyes.

A woman came out of the door to meet us. She had had time during our graceful winding approach to prepare for us. What an irrevocable vow to old maidenhood! At least twenty-five, almost a possible grandmother, according to Acadian computation, and well in the grip of advancing years. She was dressed in a stiff, dark red calico gown, with a white apron. Her black hair, smooth and glossy under a varnish of grease, was plaited high in the back, and dropped regular ringlets, six in all, over her forehead. That was the epoch when her calamity came to her, when the hair was worn in that fashion. A woman seldom alters her coiffure after a calamity of a certain nature happens to her. The figure had taken a compact rigidity, an unfaltering inflexibility, all the world away from the elasticity of matronhood; and her eyes were clear and fixed like her figure, neither falling, nor rising, nor puzzling under other eyes. Her lips, her hands, her slim feet, were conspicuously single, too, in their intent, neither reaching, nor feeling, nor running for those other lips, hands, and feet which should have doubled their single life.

That was Adorine Mérionaux, otherwise the most industrious Acadian and the best cottonade-weaver in the parish. It had been short, her story. A woman's love is still with those people her story. She was thirteen when she met him. That is the age for an Acadian girl to meet him, because, you know, the large families—the thirteen, fourteen, fifteen, twenty children—take up the years; and when one wishes to know one's great-great-grandchildren (which is the dream of the Acadian girl) one must not delay one's story.

She had one month to love him in, and in one week they were to have the wedding. The Acadians believe that marriage must come *au point*, as cooks say their sauces must be served. Standing on the bayou-bank in front of the Mérionaux, one could say "Good day" with the eyes to the Zévérin Theriots—that was the name of the parents of the young bridegroom. Looking under the branches of the oaks, one could see across the prairie,—prairie and sea-marsh it was,—

and clearly distinguish another little red-
washed house like the Mérionaux, with a
painted roof hanging over the windows, and
a staircase going up outside to the garret.
With the sun shining in the proper direction,
one might distinguish more, and with love
shining like the sun in the eyes, one might
see, one might see—a heart full.

It was only the eyes, however, which could
make such a quick voyage to the Zévérin
Theriots; a skiff had a long day's journey
to reach them. The bayou sauntered along
over the country like a negro on a Sunday's
pleasuring, trusting to God for time, and to
the devil for means.

Oh, nothing can travel quickly over a
bayou! Ask any one who has waited on a
bayou-bank for a physician or a life-and-
death message. Thought refuses to travel
and turn and double over it; thought, like the
eye, takes the shortest cut—straight over
the sea-marsh; and in the spring of the year,
when the lilies are in bloom, thought could
not take a more heavenly way, even from
beloved to beloved.

It was the week before marriage, that
week when, more than one's whole life after-

ward, one's heart feels most longing—most
—well, in fact, it was the week before marriage. From Sunday to Sunday, that was
all the time to be passed. Adorine—women
live through this week by the grace of God,
or perhaps they would be as unreasonable as
the men—Adorine could look across the
prairie to the little red roof during the day,
and could think across it during the night,
and get up before day to look across again—
longing, longing all the time. Of course
one must supply all this from one's own
imagination or experience.

But Adorine could sing, and she sang.
One might hear, in a favorable wind, a gun-
shot, or the barking of a dog from one place
to the other, so that singing, as to effect, was
nothing more than the voicing of her looking
and thinking and longing.

When one loves, it is as if everything was
known of and seen by the other; not only all
that passes in the head and heart, which
would in all conscience be more than enough
to occupy the other, but the talking, the
dressing, the conduct. It was then that the
back hair was braided and the front curled
more and more beautifully every day, and

that the calico dresses became stiffer and
stiffer, and the white crochet lace collar
broader and lower in the neck. At thirteen
she was beautiful enough to startle one, they
say, but that was nothing; she spent time and
care upon these things, as if, like other
women, her fate seriously depended upon
them. There is no self-abnegation like that
of a woman in love.

It was her singing, however, which most
showed that other existence in her existence.
When she sang at her spinning-wheel or her
loom, or knelt battling clothes on the bank
of the bayou, her lips would kiss out the
words, and the tune would rise and fall and
tremble, as if Zepherin were just across there,
anywhere; in fact, as if every blue and white
lily might hide an ear of him.

It was the time of the new moon, fortunately, when all sit up late in the country.
The family would stop in their talking about
the wedding to listen to her. She did not
know it herself, but it—the singing—was
getting louder and clearer, and, poor little
thing, it told everything. And after the
family went to bed they could still hear her,
sitting on the bank of the bayou, or up in her

window, singing and looking at the moon traveling across the lily prairie—for all its beauty and brightness no more beautiful and bright than a heart in love.

It was just past the middle of the week, a Thursday night. The moon was so bright the colors of the lilies could be seen, and the singing, so sweet, so far-reaching — it was the essence of the longing of love. Then it was that the miracle happened to her. Miracles are always happening to the Acadians. She could not sleep, she could not stay in bed. Her heart drove her to the window, and kept her there, and—among the civilized it could not take place, but here she could sing as she pleased in the middle of the night; it was nobody's affair, nobody's disturbance. "Saint Ann! Saint Joseph! Saint Mary!" She heard her song answered! She held her heart, she bent forward, she sang again. Oh, the air was full of music! It was all music! She fell on her knees; she listened, looking at the moon; and, with her face in her hands, looking at Zepherin. It was God's choir of angels, she thought, and one with a voice like Zepherin! Whenever it died away she would sing again, and again, and again—

6   "HER HEART DROVE HER TO THE WINDOW."

But the sun came, and the sun is not cre-
ated, like the moon, for lovers, and whatever
happened in the night, there was work to be
done in the day. Adorine worked like one in
a trance, her face as radiant as the upturned
face of a saint. They did not know what it
was, or rather they thought it was love. Love
is so different out there, they make all kinds
of allowances for it. But, in truth, Adorine
was still hearing her celestial voices or voice.
If the cackling of the chickens, the whir of the
spinning-wheel, or the "bum bum" of the
loom effaced it a moment, she had only to go
to some still place, round her hand over her
ear, and give the line of a song, and—it was
Zepherin—Zepherin she heard.

She walked in a dream until night. When
the moon came up she was at the window,
and still it continued, so faint, so sweet, that
answer to her song. Echo never did anything
more exquisite, but she knew nothing of such
a heathen as Echo. Human nature became
exhausted. She fell asleep where she was, in
the window, and dreamed as only a bride can
dream of her groom. When she awoke,
"Adorine! Adorine!" the beautiful angel
voices called to her; "Zepherin! Zepherin!"

she answered, as if she, too, were an angel,
signaling another angel in heaven. It was
too much. She wept, and that broke the
charm. She could hear nothing more after
that. All that day was despondency, dejection, tear-bedewed eyes, and tremulous lips,
the commonplace reaction, as all know, of
love exaltation. Adorine's family, Acadian
peasants though they were, knew as much
about it as any one else, and all that any one
knows about it is that marriage is the cure-
all, and the only cure-all, for love.

And Zepherin? A man could better describe his side of that week; for it, too, has
mostly to be described from imagination or
experience. What is inferred is that what
Adorine longed and thought and looked in
silence and resignation, according to woman's
way, he suffered equally, but in a man's way,
which is not one of silence or resignation,—at
least when one is a man of eighteen,—the last
interview, the near wedding, her beauty, his
love, her house in sight, the full moon, the
long, wakeful nights.

He took his pirogue; but the bayou played
with his impatience, maddened his passion,
bringing him so near, to meander with him

"ALL THAT DAY WAS DESPONDENCY, DEJECTION."

6*

again so far away.   There was only a short
prairie between him and ——, a prairie thick
with lily-roots—one could almost walk over
their heads, so close, and gleaming in the
moonlight.   But this is all only inference.

The pirogue was found tethered to the
paddle stuck upright in the soft bank, and—
Adorine's parents related the rest.   Nothing
else was found until the summer drought had
bared the swamp.

There was a little girl in the house when
we arrived—all else were in the field—a
stupid, solemn, pretty child, the child of a
brother.   How she kept away from Adorine,
and how much that testified!

It would have been too painful.   The little
arms around her neck, the head nestling to
her bosom, sleepily pressing against it.   And
the little one might ask to be sung to sleep.
Sung to sleep!

The little bed-chamber, with its high mat-
tressed bed, covered with the Acadian home-
spun quilt, trimmed with netting fringe, its
bit of mirror over the bureau, the bottle of
perfumed grease to keep the locks black and
glossy, the prayer-beads and blessed palms
hanging on the wall, the low, black polished

spinning-wheel, the loom,—the *métier d'Ado-rine* famed throughout the parish,—the ever goodly store of cotton and yarn hanks swinging from the ceiling, and the little square, open window which looked under the mossy oak-branches to look over the prairie; and once again all blue and white lilies—they were all there, as Adorine was there; but there was more — not there.

ANNE MARIE AND JEANNE MARIE

OLD Jeanne Marie leaned her hand against
the house, and the tears rolled down
her cheeks. She had not wept since she
buried her last child. With her it was one
trouble, one weeping, no more; and her
wrinkled, hard, polished skin so far had
known only the tears that come after death.
The trouble in her heart now was almost
exactly like the trouble caused by death;
although she knew it was not so bad as death,
yet, when she thought of this to console herself, the tears rolled all the faster. She took
the end of the red cotton kerchief tied over
her head, and wiped them away; for the fur-
rows in her face did not merely run up and
down—they ran in all directions, and carried
her tears all over her face at once. She could
understand death, but she could not understand this.

It came about in this way : Anne Marie and she lived in the little red-washed cabin against which she leaned; had lived there alone with each other for fifty years, ever since Jeanne Marie's husband had died, and the three children after him, in the fever epidemic.

The little two-roomed cabin, the stable where there used to be a cow, the patch of ground planted with onions, had all been bought and paid for by the husband; for he was a thrifty, hard-working Gascon, and had he lived there would not have been one better off, or with a larger family, either in that quarter or in any of the red-washed suburbs with which Gascony has surrounded New Orleans. His women, however,—the wife and sister-in-law,—had done their share in the work : a man's share apiece, for with the Gascon women there is no discrimination of sex when it comes to work.

And they worked on just the same after he died, tending the cow, digging, hoeing, planting, watering. The day following the funeral, by daylight Jeanne Marie was shouldering around the yoke of milk-cans to his patrons, while Anne Marie carried the vegetables to market; and so on for fifty years.

They were old women now,—seventy-five
years old,—and, as they expressed it, they
had always been twins.   In twins there is always one lucky and one unlucky one: Jeanne
Marie was the lucky one, Anne Marie the
unlucky one.   So much so, that it was even
she who had to catch the rheumatism, and to
lie now bedridden, months at a time, while
Jeanne Marie was as active in her sabots as
she had ever been.

In spite of the age of both, and the infir-
mity of one, every Saturday night there was
some little thing to put under the brick in the
hearth, for taxes and license, and the never-
to-be-forgotten funeral provision.   In the husband's time gold pieces used to go in, but they
had all gone to pay for the four funerals and
the quadrupled doctor's bill.   The women
laid in silver pieces; the coins, however, grew
smaller and smaller, and represented more
and more not so much the gain from onions
as the saving from food.

It had been explained to them how they
might, all at once, make a year's gain in the
lottery; and it had become their custom
always, at the end of every month, to put
aside one silver coin apiece, to buy a lottery

ticket with — one ticket each, not for the great, but for the twenty-five-cent, prizes. Anne Marie would buy hers round about the market; Jeanne Marie would stop anywhere along her milk course and buy hers, and they would go together in the afternoon to stand with the little crowd watching the placard upon which the winning numbers were to be written. And when they were written, it was curious, Jeanne Marie's numbers would come out twice as often as Anne Marie's. Not that she ever won anything, for she was not lucky enough to have them come out in the order to win; they only came out here and there, singly: but it was sufficient to make old Anne Marie cross and ugly for a day or two, and injure the sale of the onion-basket. When she became bedridden, Jeanne Marie bought the ticket for both, on the numbers, however, that Anne Marie gave her; and Anne Marie had to lie in bed and wait, while Jeanne Marie went out to watch the placard.

One evening, watching it, Jeanne Marie saw the ticket-agent write out the numbers as they came on her ticket, in such a way that they drew a prize — forty dollars.

When the old woman saw it she felt such a happiness; just as she used to feel in the old times right after the birth of a baby. She thought of that instantly. Without saying a word to any one, she clattered over the *banquette* as fast as she could in her sabots, to tell the good news to Anne Marie. But she did not go so fast as not to have time to dispose of her forty dollars over and over again. Forty dollars! That was a great deal of money. She had often in her mind, when she was expecting a prize, spent twenty dollars; for she had never thought it could be more than that. But forty dollars! A new gown apiece, and black silk kerchiefs to tie over their heads instead of red cotton, and the little cabin new red-washed, and soup in the pot, and a garlic sausage, and a bottle of good, costly liniment for Anne Marie's legs; and still a pile of gold to go under the hearth-brick—a pile of gold that would have made the eyes of the defunct husband glisten.

She pushed open the picket-gate, and came into the room where her sister lay in bed.

"Eh, Anne Marie, my girl," she called in her thick, pebbly voice, apparently made pur-

posely to suit her rough Gascon accent; "this
time we have caught it!"

"Whose ticket?" asked Anne Marie, instantly.

In a flash all Anne Marie's ill luck ran
through Jeanne Marie's mind; how her promised husband had proved unfaithful, and
Jeanne Marie's faithful; and how, ever since,
even to the coming out of her lottery numbers, even to the selling of vegetables, even
to the catching of the rheumatism, she had
been the loser.   But above all, as she looked
at Anne Marie in the bed, all the misery came
over Jeanne Marie of her sister's not being
able, in all her poor old seventy-five years
of life, to remember the pressure of the
arms of a husband about her waist, nor the
mouth of a child on her breast.

As soon as Anne Marie had asked her question, Jeanne Marie answered it.

"But your ticket, *Coton-Maï!*" [1]

"Where?   Give it here!   Give it here!"
The old woman, who had not been able to
move her back for weeks, sat bolt upright in
bed, and stretched out her great bony fingers,

---

[1] *Coton-Maï* is an innocent oath invented by the good, pious priest
as a substitute for one more harmful.

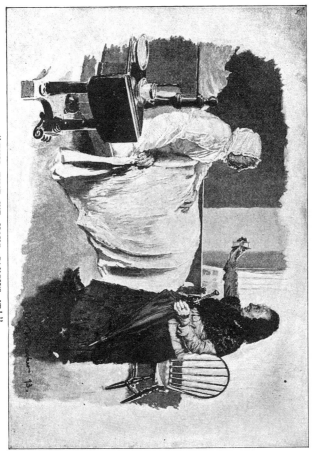

"THIS TIME WE HAVE CAUGHT IT!"

with the long nails as hard and black as
rake-prongs from groveling in the earth.

Jeanne Marie poured the money out of her
cotton handkerchief into them.

Anne Marie counted it, looked at it;
looked at it, counted it; and if she had not
been so old, so infirm, so toothless, the smile
that passed over her face would have made it
beautiful.

Jeanne Marie had to leave her to draw
water from the well to water the plants, and
to get her vegetables ready for next morning.
She felt even happier now than if she had just
had a child, happier even than if her husband
had just returned to her.

" Ill luck! *Coton-Maï!* Ill luck! There 's
a way to turn ill luck!" And her smile also
should have beautified her face, wrinkled and
ugly though it was.

She did not think any more of the spending of the money, only of the pleasure Anne
Marie would take in spending it.

The water was low in the well, and there
had been a long drought. There are not
many old women of seventy-five who could
have watered so much ground as abundantly
as she did; but whenever she thought of

the forty dollars and Anne Marie's smile
she would give the thirsting plant an extra
bucketful.

The twilight was gaining.   She paused.
" *Coton-Maï!* " she exclaimed aloud.   " But
I must see the old woman smile again over
her good luck."

Although it was " my girl " face to face, it
was always " the old woman " behind each
other's back.

There was a knot-hole in the plank walls
of the house.   In spite of Anne Marie's rheumatism they would never stop it up, needing
it, they said, for light and air.   Jeanne Marie
slipped her feet out of her sabots and crept
easily toward it, smiling, and saying " *Coton-
Maï!* " to herself all the way.   She put her
eye to the hole.   Anne Marie was not in the
bed, she who had not left her bed for two
months!   Jeanne Marie looked through the
dim light of the room until she found her.

Anne Marie, in her short petticoat and
nightsack, with bare legs and feet, was on
her knees in the corner, pulling up a plank,
hiding—peasants know hiding when they see
it—hiding her money away—away—away
from whom?—muttering to herself and shak-

ing her old grayhaired head. Hiding her
money away from Jeanne Marie!

And this was why Jeanne Marie leaned
her head against the side of the house and
wept. It seemed to her that she had never
known her twin sister at all.

A CRIPPLED HOPE

A CRIPPLED HOPE

YOU must picture to yourself the quiet, dim-lighted room of a convalescent; outside, the dreary, bleak days of winter in a sparsely settled, distant country parish; inside, a slow, smoldering log-fire, a curtained bed, the infant sleeping well enough, the mother wakeful, restless, thought-driven, as a mother must be, unfortunately, nowadays, particularly in that parish, where cotton worms and overflows have acquired such a monopoly of one's future.

God is always pretty near a sick woman's couch; but nearer even than God seems the sick-nurse — at least in that part of the country, under those circumstances. It is so good to look through the dimness and uncertainty, moral and physical, and to meet those little black, steadfast, all-seeing eyes; to feel those smooth, soft, all-soothing hands; to hear, across one's sleep, that three-footed step —

the flat-soled left foot, the tiptoe right, and the padded end of the broomstick ; and when one is so wakeful and restless and thought-driven, to have another's story given one. God, depend upon it, grows stories and lives as he does herbs, each with a mission of balm to some woe.

She said she had, and in truth she had, no other name than "little Mammy"; and that was the name of her nature. Pure African, but bronze rather than pure black, and full-sized only in width, her growth having been hampered as to height by an injury to her hip, which had lamed her, pulling her figure awry, and burdening her with a protuberance of the joint. Her mother caused it by dropping her when a baby, and concealing it, for fear of punishment, until the dislocation became irremediable. All the animosity of which little Mammy was capable centered upon this unknown but never-to-be-forgotten mother of hers ; out of this hatred had grown her love—that is, her destiny, a woman's love being her destiny. Little Mammy's love was for children.

The birth and infancy (the one as accidental as the other, one would infer) took place in—

it sounds like the "Arabian Nights" now!—
took place in the great room, caravansary,
stable, behind a negro-trader's auction-mart,
where human beings underwent literally the

"THE QUIET, DIM-LIGHTED ROOM OF A CONVALESCENT."

daily buying and selling of which the world
now complains in a figure of speech—a great,
square, dusty chamber where, sitting cross-
legged, leaning against the wall, or lying on
foul blanket pallets on the floor, the bargains

of to-day made their brief sojourn, awaiting
transformation into the profits of the morrow.

The place can be pointed out now, is often
pointed out; but no emotion arises at sight of
it.   It is so plain, so matter-of-fact an edifice
that emotion only comes afterward in thinking
about it, and then in the reflection that such
an edifice could be, then as now, plain and
matter-of-fact.

For the slave-trader there was no capital
so valuable as the physical soundness of his
stock; the moral was easily enough forged
or counterfeited.   Little Mammy's good-for-
nothing mother was sold as readily as a vote,
in the parlance of to-day; but no one would
pay for a crippled baby.   The mother herself
would not have taken her as a gift, had it
been in the nature of a negro-trader to give
away anything.   Some doctoring was done,—
so little Mammy heard traditionally,—some
effort made to get her marketable.   There
were attempts to pair her off as a twin sister
of various correspondencies in age, size, and
color, and to palm her off, as a substitute, at
migratory, bereaved, overfull breasts.   Nothing equaled a negro-trader's will and power
for fraud, except the hereditary distrust and

watchfulness which it bred and maintained.
And so, in the even balance between the two
categories, the little cripple remained a fixture
in the stream of life that passed through that

"LITTLE MAMMY."

back room, in the fluxes and refluxes of buying and selling; not valueless, however—
rely upon a negro-trader for discovering val-
ues as substitutes, as panaceas. She earned
her nourishment, and Providence did not let

it kill the little animal before the emancipation
of weaning arrived.

How much circumstances evoked, how
much instinct responded, belongs to the secrets which nature seems to intend keeping.
As a baby she had eyes, attention, solely for
other babies. One cannot say while she was
still crawling, for she could only crawl years
after she should have been walking, but, before even precocious walking-time, tradition
or the old gray-haired negro janitor relates,
she would creep from baby to baby to play
with it, put it to sleep, pat it, rub its stomach
(a negro baby, you know, is all stomach, and
generally aching stomach at that). And before she had a lap, she managed to force one
for some ailing nursling. It was then that
they began to call her "little Mammy." In
the transitory population of the "pen" no one
stayed long enough to give her another name;
and no one ever stayed short enough to give
her another one.

Her first recollection of herself was that
she could not walk—she was past crawling;
she cradled herself along, as she called sitting down flat, and working herself about
with her hands and her one strong leg.

Babbling babies walked all around her,—
many walking before they babbled,—and
still she did not walk, imitate them as she
might and did.   She would sit and "study"
about it, make another trial, fall; sit and
study some more, make another trial, fall
again.   Negroes, who believe that they must
give a reason for everything even if they
have to invent one, were convinced that it
was all this studying upon her lameness that
gave her such a large head.

And now she began secretly turning up
the clothes of every negro child that came
into that pen, and examining its legs, and
still more secretly examining her own,
stretched out before her on the ground.
How long it took she does not remember;
in fact, she could not have known, for she
had no way of measuring time except by her
thoughts and feelings.   But in her own way
and time the due process of deliberation was
fulfilled, and the quotient made clear that,
bowed or not, all children's legs were of
equal length except her own, and all were
alike, not one full, strong, hard, the other
soft, flabby, wrinkled, growing out of a knot
at the hip.   A whole psychological period

apparently lay between that conclusion and
—a broom-handle walking-stick; but the
broomstick came, as it was bound to come,—
thank heaven!—from that premise, and what
with stretching one limb to make it longer,
and doubling up the other to make it shorter,
she invented that form of locomotion which
is still carrying her through life, and with
no more exaggerated leg-crookedness than
many careless negroes born with straight
limbs display. This must have been when
she was about eight or nine. Hobbling on
a broomstick, with, no doubt, the same weird,
wizened face as now, an innate sense of the
fitness of things must have suggested the
kerchief tied around her big head, and the
burlaps rag of an apron in front of her linsey-
woolsey rag of a gown, and the bit of broken
pipe-stem in the corner of her mouth, where
the pipe should have been, and where it was
in after years. That is the way she recol-
lected herself, and that is the way one recalls
her now, with a few modifications.

The others came and went, but she was
always there. It was n't long before she became "little Mammy" to the grown folks
too; and the newest inmates soon learned to

cry: " Where 's little Mammy ? " " Oh, little
Mammy! little Mammy! Such a misery in
my head [or my back, or my stomach]!
Can't you help me, little Mammy?" It was
curious what a quick eye she had for symp-
toms and ailments, and what a quick ear for
suffering, and how apt she was at picking up,
remembering, and inventing remedies. It
never occurred to her not to crouch at the
head or the foot of a sick pallet, day and
night through. As for the nights, she said
she dared not close her eyes of nights. The
room they were in was so vast, and sometimes the negroes lay so thick on the floor,
rolled in their blankets (you know, even in
the summer they sleep under blankets), all
snoring so loudly, she would never have
heard a groan or a whimper any more than
they did, if she had slept, too. And negro
mothers are so careless and such heavy
sleepers. All night she would creep at
regular intervals to the different pallets, and
draw the little babies from under, or away
from, the heavy, inert impending mother
forms. There is no telling how many she thus
saved from being overlaid and smothered, or,
what was worse, maimed and crippled.

8

Whenever a physician came in, as he was
sometimes called, to look at a valuable invest-
ment or to furbish up some piece of damaged
goods, she always managed to get near to
hear the directions; and she generally was
the one to apply them also, for negroes always would steal medicines most scurvily
one from the other. And when death at
times would slip into the pen, despite the trader's utmost alertness and precautions,—as
death often "had to do," little Mammy said,
—when the time of some of them came to
die, and when the rest of the negroes, with
African greed of eye for the horrible, would
press around the lowly couch where the
agonizing form of a slave lay writhing out
of life, she would always to the last give
medicines, and wipe the cold forehead, and
soothe the clutching, fearsome hands, hop-
ing to the end, and trying to inspire the
hope that his or her "time" had not come
yet; for, as she said, " Our time does n't
come just as often as it does come."

And in those sad last offices, which some-
how have always been under reproach as a
kind of shame, no matter how young she
was, she was always too old to have the

childish avoidance of them. On the con-
trary, to her a corpse was only a kind of
baby, and she always strove, she said, to
make one, like the other, easy and comfortable.

And in other emergencies she divined the
mysteries of the flesh, as other precocities
divine the mysteries of painting and music,
and so become child wonders.

Others came and went. She alone remained there. Babies of her babyhood—
the toddlers she, a toddler, had nursed—
were having babies themselves now; the middle-aged had had time to grow old and die.
Every week new families were coming into
the great back chamber; every week they
passed out: babies, boys, girls, buxom wen-
ches, stalwart youths, and the middle-aged
—the grave, serious ones whom misfortune
had driven from their old masters, and the
ill-reputed ones, the trickish, thievish, lazy,
whom the cunning of the negro-trader alone
could keep in circulation. All were marketable, all were bought and sold, all passed in
one door and out the other—all except her,
little Mammy. As with her lameness, it took
time for her to recognize, to understand, the

fact. She could study over her lameness, she could in the dull course of time think out the broomstick way of palliation. It would have been almost better, under the circumstances, for God to have kept the truth from her; only —God keeps so little of the truth from us women. It is his system.

Poor little thing ! It was not now that her master *could* not sell her, but he *would* not! Out of her own intelligence she had forged her chains; the lameness was a hobble merely in comparison. She had become too valuable to the negro-trader by her services among his crew, and offers only solidified his determination not to sell her. Visiting physicians, after short acquaintance with her capacities, would offer what were called fancy prices for her. Planters who heard of her through their purchases would come to the city purposely to secure, at any cost, so inestimable an adjunct to their plantations. Even ladies—refined, delicate ladies—sometimes came to the pen personally to back money with influence. In vain. Little Mammy was worth more to the negro-trader, simply as a kind of insurance against accidents, than any sum, however glittering the figure, and he was no ignorant expert in human wares. She can tell it; no one else can for her. Remember that at times she had seen the streets outside. Remember that she could hear of the outside world daily from the passing chattels—of the plantations, farms, families; the green fields, Sunday woods, running streams; the camp-meetings, corn-shuckings, cotton-pickings, sugar-grindings; the baptisms, marriages, funerals, prayer-meetings; the holidays and holy days. Remember that, whether for liberty or whether for love, passion effloresces in the human being—no matter when, where, or how—with every spring's return. Remember that she was, even in middle age, young and vigorous. But no; do not remember anything. There is no need to heighten the coloring.

It would be tedious to relate, although it was not tedious to hear her relate it, the desperations and hopes of her life then. Hardly a day passed that she did not see, looking for purchases (rummaging among goods on a counter for bargains), some master whom she could have loved, some mistress whom she could have adored. Always her favorite mistresses were there—tall, delicate matrons,

8*

who came themselves, with great fatigue, to
select kindly-faced women for nurses; lan-
guid-looking ladies with smooth hair standing out in wide *bandeaux* from their heads,
and lace shawls dropping from their sloping
shoulders, silk dresses carelessly held up in
thumb and finger from embroidered petticoats
that were spread out like tents over huge
hoops which covered whole groups of swarming piccaninnies on the dirty floor; ladies, pale
from illnesses that she might have nursed,
and over-burdened with children whom she
might have reared! And not a lady of that
kind saw her face but wanted her, yearned
for her, pleaded for her, coming back secretly
to slip silver, and sometimes gold, pieces into
her hand, patting her turbaned head, calling
her "little Mammy" too, instantly, by inspiration, and making the negro-trader give them,
with all sorts of assurances, the refusal of her.
She had no need for the whispered "Buy me,
master!" "Buy me, mistress!" "You 'll see
how I can work, master!" "You 'll never be
sorry, mistress!" of the others. The negro-
trader—like hangmen, negro-traders are fitted by nature for their profession—it came
into his head—he had no heart, not even

a negro-trader's heart—that it would be more judicious to seclude her during these shopping visits, so to speak. She could not have had any hopes then at all; it must have been all desperations.

That auction-block, that executioner's block, about which so much has been written—Jacob's ladder, in his dream, was nothing to what that block appeared nightly in her dreams to her; and the climbers up and down —well, perhaps Jacob's angels were his hopes, too.

At times she determined to depreciate her usefulness, mar her value, by renouncing her heart, denying her purpose. For days she would tie her kerchief over her ears and eyes, and crouch in a corner, strangling her impulses. She even malingered, refused food, became dumb. And she might have succeeded in making herself salable through incipient lunacy, if through no other way, had she been able to maintain her rôle long enough. But some woman or baby always was falling into some emergency of pain and illness.

How it might have ended one does not like to think. Fortunately, one does not need to think.

There came a night. She sat alone in the
vast, dark caravansary — alone for the first
time in her life. Empty rags and blankets lay
strewn over the floor, no snoring, no tossing
in them more.   A sacrificial sale that day had
cleared the counters. Alarm-bells rang in the
streets, but she did not know them for alarm-
bells; alarm brooded in the dim space around
her, but she did not even recognize that. Her
protracted tension of heart had made her fear-
blind to all but one peradventure.

Once or twice she forgot herself, and
limped over to some heap to relieve an imaginary struggling babe or moaning sleeper.
Morning came. She had dozed. She looked
to see the rag-heaps stir; they lay as still as
corpses. The alarm-bells had ceased. She
looked to see a new gang enter the far door.
She listened for the gathering buzzing of
voices in the next room, around the auction-
block. She waited for the trader. She
waited for the janitor. At nightfall a file of
soldiers entered. They drove her forth,
ordering her in the voice, in the tone, of the
negro-trader. That was the only familiar
thing in the chaos of incomprehensibility
about her. She hobbled through the auction-

room. Posters, advertisements, papers, lay
on the floor, and in the torch-light glared
from the wall. Her Jacob's ladder, her step-
ping-stone to her hopes, lay overturned in
a corner.

You divine it. The negro-trader's trade
was abolished, and he had vanished in the din
and smoke of a war which he had not been
entirely guiltless of producing, leaving little
Mammy locked up behind him. Had he forgotten her? One cannot even hope so. She
hobbled out into the street, leaning on her
nine-year-old broomstick (she had grown
only slightly beyond it; could still use it by
bending over it), her head tied in a rag kerchief, a rag for a gown, a rag for an apron.

Free, she was free! But she had not hoped
for freedom. The plantation, the household,
the delicate ladies, the teeming children,—
broomsticks they were in comparison to freedom, but,—that was what she had asked,
what she had prayed for. God, she said, had
let her drop, just as her mother had done.
More than ever she grieved, as she crept
down the street, that she had never mounted
the auctioneer's block. An ownerless free
negro! She knew no one whose duty it was

to help her; no one knew her to help her. In the whole world (it was all she had asked) there was no white child to call her mammy, no white lady or gentleman (it was the extent of her dreams) beholden to her as to a nurse. And all her innumerable black beneficiaries! Even the janitor, whom she had tended as the others, had deserted her like his white prototype.

She tried to find a place for herself, but she had no indorsers, no recommenders. She dared not mention the name of the negro-trader; it banished her not only from the households of the whites, but from those of the genteel of her own color. And everywhere soldiers sentineled the streets—soldiers whose tone and accent reminded her of the negro-trader.

Her sufferings, whether imaginary or real, were sufficiently acute to drive her into the only form of escape which once had been possible to friendless negroes. She became a runaway. With a bundle tied to the end of a stick over her shoulder, just as the old prints represent it, she fled from her homelessness and loneliness, from her ignoble past, and the heart-disappointing termination of it. Following a railroad track, journeying afoot, sleep-

ing by the roadside, she lived on until she
came to the one familiar landmark in life to
her — a sick woman, but a white one. And
so, progressing from patient to patient (it was
a time when sick white women studded the
country like mile-posts), she arrived at a little
town, a kind of a refuge for soldiers' wives and
widows. She never traveled further. She
could not. Always, as in the pen, some
emergency of pain and illness held her.

That is all. She is still there. The poor,
poor women of that stricken region say that
little Mammy was the only alleviation God
left them after Sheridan passed through; and
the richer ones say very much the same
thing —

But one should hear her tell it herself, as
has been said, on a cold, gloomy winter day
in the country, the fire glimmering on the
hearth; the overworked husband in the fields;
the baby quiet at last; the mother uneasy,
restless, thought-driven; the soft black hand
rubbing backward and forward, rubbing out
aches and frets and nervousness.

The eyelids droop; the firelight plays fan-
tasies on the bed-curtains; the ear drops
words, sentences; one gets confused — one
sleeps — one dreams.

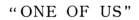

"ONE OF US"

"ONE OF US"

AT the first glance one might have been inclined to doubt; but at the second anybody would have recognized her—that is, with a little mental rehabilitation: the bright little rouge spots in the hollow of her cheek, the eyebrows well accentuated with paint, the thin lips rose-tinted, and the dull, straight hair frizzed and curled and twisted and turned by that consummate rascal and artist, the official beautifier and rectifier of stage humanity, Robert, the opera *coiffeur*. Who in the world knows better than he the gulf between the real and the ideal, the limitations between the natural and the romantic?

Yes, one could see her, in that time-honored thin silk dress of hers stiffened into brocade by buckram underneath; the high, low-necked waist, hiding any evidences of breast, if there were such evidences to hide, and bringing the long neck into such faulty prominence; and the sleeves, crisp puffs of tulle divided by bands of red velvet, through which the poor lean arm runs like a wire, stringing them together like beads. Yes, it was she, the whilom *dugazon* of the opera troupe. Not that she ever was a *dugazon*, but that was what her voice once aspired to be: a *dugazon manquée* would better describe her.

What a ghost! But they always appeared like mere evaporations of real women. For what woman of flesh and blood can seriously maintain through life the rôle of sham attendant on sham sensations, and play public celebrant of other women's loves and lovers, singing, or rather saying, nothing more enlivening than: "Oh, madame!" and "Ah, madame!" and "*Quelle ivresse!*" or "*Quelle horreur!*" or, in recitative, detailing whatever dreary platitudes and inanities the librettist and Heaven connive to put upon the tongues of confidantes and attendants?

Looking at her—how it came over one! The music, the lights, the scene; the fat soprano confiding to her the fact of the "amour extrême" she bears for the tenor, to which

"TO POSE IN ABJECT PATIENCE AND AWKWARDNESS."

she, the *dugazon*, does not even try to listen;
her eyes wandering listlessly over the audience. The calorous secret out, and in her
possession, how she stumbles over her train
to the back of the stage, there to pose in
abject patience and awkwardness, while the
gallant barytone, touching his sword, and
flinging his cape over his shoulder, defies the
world and the tenor, who is just recovering
from his "ut de poitrine" behind the scenes.

She was talking to me all the time, apolo-
gizing for the intrusion, explaining her mission, which involved a short story of her life,
as women's intrusions and missions usually
do. But my thoughts, also as usual, distracted me from listening, as so often they
have distracted me from following what was
perhaps more profitable.

The composer, of course, wastes no music
upon her; flinging to her only an occasional
recitative in two notes, but always ending in
a reef of a scale, trill, or roulade, for her
to wreck her voice on before the audience.
The *chef d' orchestre*, if he is charitable,
starts her off with a contribution from his
own lusty lungs, and then she—oh, her voice
is always thinner and more osseous than her

arms, and her smile no more graceful than
her train !

As well think of the simulated trees, water-
falls, and châteaux leaving the stage, as the
dugazon ! One always imagines them singing on into dimness, dustiness, unsteadiness,
and uselessness, until, like any other piece
of stage property, they are at last put
aside and simply left there at the end of
some season — there seems to be a super-
stition against selling or burning useless and
dilapidated stage property. As it came to
me, the idea was not an impossibility. The
last representation of the season is over.
She, tired beyond judgment — haply, beyond
feeling — by her tireless rôle, sinks upon her
chair to rest in her dressing-room ; sinks,
further, to sleep. She has no maid. The
troupe, hurrying away to France on the
special train waiting not half a dozen blocks
away, forget her — the insignificant are so
easily forgotten ! The porter, more tired,
perhaps, than any one of the beautiful ideal
world about him, and savoring already in
advance the good onion-flavored *grillade*
awaiting him at home, locks up everything
fast and tight ; the tighter and faster for the

good fortnight's vacation he has promised himself.

No doubt if the old opera-house were ever cleaned out, just such a heap of stiff, wire-strung bones would be found, in some such hole as the *dugazon's* dressing-room, desic-cating away in its last costume — perhaps in that very costume of *Inez;* and if one were venturesome enough to pass Allhallowe'en there, the spirit of those bones might be seen availing itself of the privilege of unasperged corpses to roam. Not singing, not talking — it is an anachronism to say that ghosts talk: their medium of communication must be pure thought; and one should be able to see their thoughts working, just as one sees the work-ing of the digestive organs in the clear vis-cera of transparent animalculæ. The hard thing of it is that ghosts are chained to the same scenes that chained their bodies, and when they sleep-walk, so to speak, it must be through phases of former existence. What a nightmare for them to go over once again the lived and done, the suffered and finished! What a comfort to wake up and find one's self dead, well dead!

I could have continued and put the whole

9*

opera troupe in "costume de ghost," but I
think it was the woman's eyes that drew me
back to her face and her story. She had a
sensible face, now that I observed her naturally, as it were; and her hands,—how I have
agonized over those hands on the stage!—
all knuckles and exaggerated veins, clutching her dress as she sang, or, petrified,
outstretched to *Leonore's* "Pourquoi ces
larmes?"—her hands were the hands of an
honest, hard-working woman who buckrams
her own skirts, and at need could scrub her
own floor. Her face (my description following my wandering glance)— her face was
careworn, almost to desuetude; not dissipa-
tion-worn, as, alas! the faces of the more
gifted ladies of opera troupes too often are.
There was no fattening in it of pastry, truf-
fles, and bonbons; upon it none of the tracery
left by nightly champagne tides and ripples;
and consequently her figure, under her plain
dress, had not that for display which the
world has conventioned to call charms.
Where a window-cord would hardly have
sufficed to girdle *Leonore*, a necklace would
have served her. She had not beauty
enough to fear the flattering dangers of

masculine snares and temptations,—or there
may have been other reasons,—but as a
wife—there was something about her that
guaranteed it—she would have blossomed
love and children as a fig-tree does figs.

In truth, she was just talking about children. The first part of her story had passed:
her birthplace, education, situation; and now
she was saying:

"I have always had the temptation, but
I have always resisted it. Now,"—with a
blush at her excuse,—"it may be your spring
weather, your birds, your flowers, your sky—
and your children in the streets. The longing
came over me yesterday: I thought of it on
the stage, I thought of it afterward—it was
better than sleeping; and this morning"—
her eyes moistened, she breathed excitedly
—"I was determined. I gave up, I made
inquiry, I was sent to you. Would it be
possible? Would there be any place" ("any
rôle," she said first) "in any of your asylums,
in any of your charitable institutions, for me?
I would ask nothing but my clothes and food,
and very little of that; the recompense would
be the children—the little girl children,"
with a smile—can you imagine the smile of

a woman dreaming of children that might
be? "Think! Never to have held a child in
my arms more than a moment, never to have
felt a child's arms about my neck! Never to
have known a child! Born on a stage, my
mother born on a stage!" Ah, there were
tragic possibilities in that voice and movement! "Pardon, madam. You see how I
repeat. And you must be very wearied
hearing about me. But I could be their
nurse and their servant. I would bathe and
dress them, play with them, teach them their
prayers; and when they are sick they would
see no difference. They would not know but
what their mother was there!"

Oh, she had her program all prepared;
one could see that.

"And I would sing to them—no! no!"
with a quick gesture, "nothing from the
stage; little songs and lullabys I have picked
up traveling around, and," hesitating, "little
things I have composed myself—little things
that I thought children would like to hear
some day." What did she not unconsciously
throw into those last words? "I dream of
it," she pursued, talking with as little regard
to me as on the stage she sang to the

prima donna. "Their little arms, their little faces, their little lips! And in an asylum there would be so many of them! When they cried and were in trouble I would take them in my lap, and I would say to them, with all sorts of tenderness—" She had arranged that in her program, too—all the minutiæ of what she would say to them in their distress. But women are that way. When once they begin to love, their hearts are magnifying-lenses for them to feel through. "And my heart hungers to commence right here, now, at once! It seems to me I cannot wait. Ah, madam, no more stage, no more opera!" speaking quickly, feverishly. "As I said, it may be your beautiful spring, your flowers, your birds, and your numbers of children. I have always loved that place most where there are most children; and you have more children here than I ever saw anywhere. Children are so beautiful! It is strange, is it not, when you consider my life and my rearing?"

Her life, her rearing, how interesting they must have been! What a pity I had not listened more attentively!

"They say you have much to do with asylums here."

Evidently, when rôles do not exist in life for certain characters, God has to create them. And thus He had to create a rôle in an asylum for my friend, for so she became from the instant she spoke of children as she did. It was the poorest and neediest of asylums; and the poor little orphaned wretches—but it is better not to speak of them. How can God ever expect to rear children without their mothers!

But the rôle I craved to create for my friend was far different—some good, honest bourgeois interior, where lips are coarse and cheeks are ruddy, and where life is composed of real scenes, set to the real music of life, the homely successes and failures, and loves and hates, and embraces and tears, that fill out the orchestra of the heart; where romance and poetry abound *au naturel;* and where— yes, where children grow as thick as nature permits: the domestic interior of the opera porter, for instance, or the clockmaker over the way. But what a loss the orphan-asylum would have suffered, and the dreary lacking there would have been in the lives of the

children ! For there must have been moments
in the lives of the children in that asylum
when they felt, awake, as they felt in their
sleep when they dreamed their mothers were
about them.

THE LITTLE CONVENT GIRL

THE LITTLE CONVENT GIRL

SHE was coming down on the boat from Cincinnati, the little convent girl. Two sisters had brought her aboard. They gave her in charge of the captain, got her a state-room, saw that the new little trunk was put into it, hung the new little satchel up on the wall, showed her how to bolt the door at night, shook hands with her for good-by (good-bys have really no significance for sisters), and left her there. After a while the bells all rang, and the boat, in the awkward elephantine fashion of boats, got into midstream. The chambermaid found her sitting on the chair in the state-room where the sisters had left her, and showed her how to sit on a chair in the saloon. And there she sat until the captain came and hunted her up for supper. She could not do anything of herself; she had to be initiated into everything by some one else.

She was known on the boat only as "the little convent girl." Her name, of course, was registered in the clerk's office, but on a steamboat no one thinks of consulting the clerk's ledger. It is always the little widow, the fat madam, the tall colonel, the parson, etc. The captain, who pronounced by the letter, always called her the little con*vent* girl. She was the beau-ideal of the little convent girl. She never raised her eyes except when spoken to. Of course she never spoke first, even to the chambermaid, and when she did speak it was in the wee, shy, furtive voice one might imagine a just-budding violet to have; and she walked with such soft, easy, carefully calculated steps that one naturally felt the penalties that must have secured them—penalties dictated by a black code of deportment.

She was dressed in deep mourning. Her black straw hat was trimmed with stiff new crape, and her stiff new bombazine dress had crape collar and cuffs. She wore her hair in two long plaits fastened around her head tight and fast. Her hair had a strong inclination to curl, but that had been taken out of it as austerely as the noise out of her footfalls.

THE SISTERS BID HER GOOD-BY.

Her hair was as black as her dress; her
eyes, when one saw them, seemed blacker
than either, on account of the bluishness of
the white surrounding the pupil.   Her eye-
lashes were almost as thick as the black veil
which the sisters had fastened around her hat
with an extra pin the very last thing before
leaving.   She had a round little face, and a
tiny pointed chin; her mouth was slightly
protuberant from the teeth, over which she
tried to keep her lips well shut, the effort
giving them a pathetic little forced expression.   Her complexion was sallow, a pale
sallow, the complexion of a brunette bleached
in darkened rooms.   The only color about
her was a blue taffeta ribbon from which
a large silver medal of the Virgin hung over
the place where a breastpin should have been.
She was so little, so little, although she was
eighteen, as the sisters told the captain;
otherwise they would not have permitted her
to travel all the way to New Orleans alone.

Unless the captain or the clerk remembered to fetch her out in front, she would sit
all day in the cabin, in the same place,
crocheting lace, her spool of thread and box
of patterns in her lap, on the handkerchief

spread to save her new dress. Never leaning back—oh, no! always straight and stiff, as if the conventual back board were there within call. She would eat only convent fare at first, notwithstanding the importunities of the waiters, and the jocularities of the captain, and particularly of the clerk. Every one knows the fund of humor possessed by a steamboat clerk, and what a field for display the table at meal-times affords. On Friday she fasted rigidly, and she never began to eat, or finished, without a little Latin movement of the lips and a sign of the cross. And always at six o'clock of the evening she remembered the angelus, although there was no church bell to remind her of it.

She was in mourning for her father, the sisters told the captain, and she was going to New Orleans to her mother. She had not seen her mother since she was an infant, on account of some disagreement between the parents, in consequence of which the father had brought her to Cincinnati, and placed her in the convent. There she had been for twelve years, only going to her father for vacations and holidays. So long as the father lived he would never let the child have any communication with her mother. Now that he was dead all that was changed, and the first thing that the girl herself wanted to do was to go to her mother.

The mother superior had arranged it all with the mother of the girl, who was to come personally to the boat in New Orleans, and receive her child from the captain, presenting a letter from the mother superior, a facsimile of which the sisters gave the captain.

It is a long voyage from Cincinnati to New Orleans, the rivers doing their best to make it interminable, embroidering themselves *ad libitum* all over the country. Every five miles, and sometimes oftener, the boat would stop to put off or take on freight, if not both. The little convent girl, sitting in the cabin, had her terrible frights at first from the hideous noises attendant on these landings—the whistles, the ringings of the bells, the running to and fro, the shouting. Every time she thought it was shipwreck, death, judgment, purgatory; and her sins! her sins! She would drop her crochet, and clutch her prayer-beads from her pocket, and relax the constraint over her lips, which would go to rattling off prayers with the ve-

10*

locity of a relaxed windlass. That was at
first, before the captain took to fetching her
out in front to see the boat make a landing.

WATCHING A LANDING.

Then she got to liking it so much that she
would stay all day just where the captain put
her, going inside only for her meals. She

forgot herself at times so much that she
would draw her chair a little closer to the
railing, and put up her veil, actually, to see
better.   No one ever usurped her place,
quite in front, or intruded upon her either
with word or look; for every one learned to
know her shyness, and began to feel a personal interest in her, and all wanted the
little convent girl to see everything that
she possibly could.

And it was worth seeing—the balancing
and *chasséeing* and waltzing of the cumber-
some old boat to make a landing.   It seemed
to be always attended with the difficulty and
the improbability of a new enterprise; and
the relief when it did sidle up anywhere
within rope's-throw of the spot aimed at!
And the roustabout throwing the rope from
the perilous end of the dangling gang-plank!
And the dangling roustabouts hanging like
drops of water from it—dropping sometimes
twenty feet to the land, and not infrequently
into the river itself.   And then what a rolling of barrels, and shouldering of sacks, and
singing of Jim Crow songs, and pacing of
Jim Crow steps; and black skins glistening
through torn shirts, and white teeth gleaming

through red lips, and laughing, and talking
and—bewildering! entrancing! Surely the
little convent girl in her convent walls never
dreamed of so much unpunished noise and
movement in the world!

The first time she heard the mate—it must
have been like the first time woman ever
heard man—curse and swear, she turned
pale, and ran quickly, quickly into the saloon,
and—came out again? No, indeed! not with
all the soul she had to save, and all the other
sins on her conscience. She shook her head
resolutely, and was not seen in her chair
on deck again until the captain not only re-
assured her, but guaranteed his reassurance.
And after that, whenever the boat was about
to make a landing, the mate would first
glance up to the guards, and if the little convent girl was sitting there he would change
his invective to sarcasm, and politely request
the colored gentlemen not to hurry themselves—on no account whatever; to take
their time about shoving out the plank; to
send the rope ashore by post-office—write
him when it got there; begging them not
to strain their backs; calling them mister,
colonel, major, general, prince, and your royal

highness, which was vastly amusing. At
night, however, or when the little convent
girl was not there, language flowed in its
natural curve, the mate swearing like a
pagan to make up for lost time.

The captain forgot himself one day: it was
when the boat ran aground in the most un-
expected manner and place, and he went to
work to express his opinion, as only steamboat
captains can, of the pilot, mate, engineer, crew,
boat, river, country, and the world in general,
ringing the bell, first to back, then to head,
shouting himself hoarser than his own whistle
—when he chanced to see the little black
figure hurrying through the chaos on the
deck; and the captain stuck as fast aground
in midstream as the boat had done.

In the evening the little convent girl would
be taken on the upper deck, and going up
the steep stairs there was such confusion, to
keep the black skirts well over the stiff white
petticoats; and, coming down, such blushing
when suspicion would cross the unprepared
face that a rim of white stocking might be
visible; and the thin feet, laced so tightly in
the glossy new leather boots, would cling to
each successive step as if they could never,

never make another venture; and then one
boot would (there is but that word) hesitate
out, and feel and feel around, and have such a
pause of helpless agony as if indeed the next
step must have been wilfully removed, or was
nowhere to be found on the wide, wide earth.

It was a miracle that the pilot ever got
her up into the pilot-house; but pilots have
a lonely time, and do not hesitate even at
miracles when there is a chance for company.
He would place a box for her to climb to the
tall bench behind the wheel, and he would
arrange the cushions, and open a window
here to let in air, and shut one there to cut
off a draft, as if there could be no tenderer
consideration in life for him than her comfort.
And he would talk of the river to her, explain
the chart, pointing out eddies, whirlpools,
shoals, depths, new beds, old beds, cut-offs,
caving banks, and making banks, as exquisitely and respectfully as if she had been
the River Commission.

It was his opinion that there was as great
a river as the Mississippi flowing directly
under it—an underself of a river, as much a
counterpart of the other as the second story
of a house is of the first; in fact, he said they

were navigating through the upper story.
Whirlpools were holes in the floor of the
upper river, so to speak; eddies were rifts
and cracks. And deep under the earth,
hurrying toward the subterranean stream,
were other streams, small and great, but all
deep, hurrying to and from that great mother-
stream underneath, just as the small and great
overground streams hurry to and from their
mother Mississippi. It was almost more than
the little convent girl could take in: at least
such was the expression of her eyes; for they
opened as all eyes have to open at pilot
stories. And he knew as much of astronomy
as he did of hydrology, could call the stars
by name, and define the shapes of the con-
stellations; and she, who had studied astronomy at the convent, was charmed to find
that what she had learned was all true. It
was in the pilot-house, one night, that she
forgot herself for the first time in her life, and
stayed up until after nine o'clock. Although
she appeared almost intoxicated at the wild
pleasure, she was immediately overwhelmed
at the wickedness of it, and observed much
more rigidity of conduct thereafter. The
engineer, the boiler-men, the firemen, the

stokers, they all knew when the little convent
girl was up in the pilot-house: the speaking-
tube became so mild and gentle.

With all the delays of river and boat, however, there is an end to the journey from Cincinnati to New Orleans. The latter city,
which at one time to the impatient seemed
at the terminus of the never, began, all of a
sudden, one day to make its nearingness felt;
and from that period every other interest
paled before the interest in the immanence
of arrival into port, and the whole boat was
seized with a panic of preparation, the little
convent girl with the others. Although so
immaculate was she in person and effects that
she might have been struck with a landing,
as some good people might be struck with
death, at any moment without fear of results,
her trunk was packed and repacked, her
satchel arranged and rearranged, and, the last
day, her hair was brushed and plaited and
smoothed over and over again until the very
last glimmer of a curl disappeared. Her dress
was whisked, as if for microscopic inspection;
her face was washed; and her finger-nails
were scrubbed with the hard convent nail-
brush, until the disciplined little tips ached

with a pristine soreness. And still there were
hours to wait, and still the boat added up
delays. But she arrived at last, after all, with
not more than the usual and expected difference between the actual and the advertised
time of arrival.

There was extra blowing and extra ringing,
shouting, commanding, rushing up the gangway and rushing down the gangway. The
clerks, sitting behind tables on the first deck,
were plied, in the twinkling of an eye, with
estimates, receipts, charges, countercharges,
claims, reclaims, demands, questions, accusa-
tions, threats, all at topmost voices. None but
steamboat clerks could have stood it. And
there were throngs composed of individuals
every one of whom wanted to see the captain
first and at once: and those who could not get
to him shouted over the heads of the others;
and as usual he lost his temper and politeness,
and began to do what he termed "hustle."

"Captain! Captain!" a voice called him to
where a hand plucked his sleeve, and a letter
was thrust toward him. "The cross, and the
name of the convent." He recognized the en-
velop of the mother superior. He read the
duplicate of the letter given by the sisters.

He looked at the woman—the mother—
casually, then again and again.

The little convent girl saw him coming,
leading some one toward her. She rose. The
captain took her hand first, before the other
greeting, " Good-by, my dear," he said. He
tried to add something else, but seemed un-
determined what. " Be a good little girl—"
It was evidently all he could think of. Nod-
ding to the woman behind him, he turned on
his heel, and left.

One of the deck-hands was sent to fetch
her trunk. He walked out behind them,
through the cabin, and the crowd on deck,
down the stairs, and out over the gangway.
The little convent girl and her mother went
with hands tightly clasped. She did not turn
her eyes to the right or left, or once (what
all passengers do) look backward at the boat
which, however slowly, had carried her surely
over dangers that she wot not of. All looked
at her as she passed. All wanted to say good-
by to the little convent girl, to see the mother
who had been deprived of her so long. Some
expressed surprise in a whistle; some in other
ways. All exclaimed audibly, or to themselves, " Colored!"

It takes about a month to make the round trip from New Orleans to Cincinnati and back, counting five days' stoppage in New Orleans. It was a month to a day when the steamboat came puffing and blowing up to the wharf again, like a stout dowager after too long a walk; and the same scene of confusion was enacted, as it had been enacted twelve times a year, at almost the same wharf for twenty years; and the same calm, a death calmness by contrast, followed as usual the next morning.

The decks were quiet and clean; one cargo had just been delivered, part of another stood ready on the levee to be shipped. The captain was there waiting for his business to begin, the clerk was in his office getting his books ready, the voice of the mate could be heard below, mustering the old crew out and a new crew in; for if steamboat crews have a single principle,—and there are those who deny them any,—it is never to ship twice in succession on the same boat. It was too early yet for any but roustabouts, marketers, and church-goers; so early that even the river was still partly mist-covered; only in places could the swift, dark current be seen rolling swiftly along.

"Captain!" A hand plucked at his elbow, as if not confident that the mere calling would secure attention. The captain turned. The mother of the little convent girl stood there, and she held the little convent girl by the hand. "I have brought her to see you," the woman said. "You were so kind—and she is so quiet, so still, all the time, I thought it would do her a pleasure."

She spoke with an accent, and with embarrassment; otherwise one would have said that she was bold and assured enough.

"She don't go nowhere, she don't do nothing but make her crochet and her prayers, so I thought I would bring her for a little visit of 'How d' ye do' to you."

There was, perhaps, some inflection in the woman's voice that might have made known, or at least awakened, the suspicion of some latent hope or intention, had the captain's ear been fine enough to detect it. There might have been something in the little convent girl's face, had his eye been more sensitive— a trifle paler, maybe, the lips a little tighter drawn, the blue ribbon a shade faded. He may have noticed that, but— And the visit of "How d' ye do" came to an end.

They walked down the stairway, the woman in front, the little convent girl—her hand released to shake hands with the captain—following, across the bared deck, out to the gangway, over to the middle of it. No one was looking, no one saw more than a flutter of white petticoats, a show of white stockings, as the little convent girl went under the water.

The roustabout dived, as the roustabouts always do, after the drowning, even at the risk of their good-for-nothing lives. The mate himself jumped overboard; but she had gone down in a whirlpool. Perhaps, as the pilot had told her whirlpools always did, it may have carried her through to the underground river, to that vast, hidden, dark Mississippi that flows beneath the one we see; for her body was never found.

GRANDMOTHER'S GRANDMOTHER

GRANDMOTHER'S GRANDMOTHER

AS the grandmother related it fresh from the primeval sources that feed a grandmother's memory, it happened thus:

In the early days of the settlement of Georgia—ah, how green and rustic appears to us now the world in the early days of the settlement of Georgia! Sometimes to women, listening to the stories of their grandmothers, it seems better to have lived then than now —her grandmother was at that time a young wife. It was the day of arduous, if not of long, courtship before marriage, when every wedding celebrated the close of an original romance ; and when young couples, for bridal trips, went out to settle new States, riding on a pillion generally, with their trousseaux following as best they could on sumpter mules ; to hear the grandmother describe it made one long to be a bride of those days.

The young husband had the enumeration
of qualities that went to the making of a man
of that period, and if the qualities were in the
proportion of ten physical to one intellectual,
it does not follow that the grandmother's
grandfather was not a man of parts. For, to
obtain the hand of his bride, an only child
and an heiress, he had to give test of his
mettle by ignoring his fortune, studying law,
and getting his license before marriage, and
binding himself to live the first year afterward on the proceeds of his practice; a device
of the time thought to be a wholesome cor-
rective of the corrupting influence of over-
wealth in young domesticities.

Although he had already chosen the sea
for his profession, and was a midshipman at
the time, with more of a reputation for living
than for learning, such was he, and such, it
may be said, was the incentive genius of his
choice, that almost before his resignation as
midshipman was accepted, his license as a
lawyer was signed. As for practice, it was
currently remarked at his wedding, at the
sight of him flying down the room in the reel
with his bride for partner, that his tongue
was as nimble as his heels, and that if he only

turned his attention to criminal practice, there
was no man in the country who would make
a better prosecuting attorney for the State.
And with him for prosecuting attorney, it
was warranted that sirrahs the highwaymen
would not continue to hold Georgia judge-
and-jury justice in quite such contemptible
estimation, and that the gallows would not be
left so long bereft of their legitimate swing-
ings. As for fees, it was predicted that
the young fellow as he stood, or rather
"chassé'd," could snap his fingers at both his
and his bride's trustees.

He did turn his attention to criminal law,
was made prosecuting attorney for the State
in his county, and, before his six months had
passed, was convincing the hitherto high and
mighty, lordly, independent knights of the
road that other counties in Georgia furnished
more secure pasturage for them.

It was a beautiful spring morning. The
young wife bade him a hearty good-by, and
stood in the doorway watching him, gay and
debonair, riding off, on his stout black
charger Beetle, in the direction of the town
in which court was to be held that week.

She herself feeling as full of ambition and

work as if she also were prosecuting attorney, with a perennial spring of eloquence bubbling in her brain, turned to her domestic duties, and, without going into the detail of them, it suffices to say that, according to the grand-mother's estimation, one morning's list of duties for a healthy young bride of that period would shame the week's work of a syndicate of them to-day. Finding herself nearing the limit of diminution of several household necessities, and the spring sug-gesting the beginning of new ones, she made up her mind to profit by her husband's absence and the fair weather to make a trad-ing visit to the neighboring town next day.

So, early in a morning as beautiful as the preceding one, mounted on her own stanch mare Maid Marion, she ambled down the green over-hung forest-road, in the vista of which she had watched her husband disappear the day before; thinking about what she had to buy, and thinking, no doubt, much more, as brides will, of the absent lord and master —as brides of those days loved to consider and denominate their husbands.

Coming into the little town, the freshly painted, swinging sign-board of the new tav-

"TURNED TO HER DOMESTIC DUTIES."

ern, "The Honest Georgian," as usual was
the thing to catch her eye; but the instant
after what should she see but Black Beetle
hitched to the rack under the tree that shad-
owed the hostelry!

It was not decorous; but she was young,
and the day of her first separation from her
husband had been so long; and was he not
also, against the firmest of resolutions and
plans, hastening back to her, the separation
being too long for him also?

Slipping her foot from the stirrup, she
jumped to the ground, and ran into the tavern.
There he stood calling hastily for a drink;
and her heart more than her eyes took in his,
to her, consecrated signalment—the riding-
boots, short clothes, blue coat, cocked hat,
ruffles. She crept up behind to surprise him,
her face, with its delight and smiles, beyond
her control. She crept, until she saw his
watch-fob dangling against the counter, and
then her heart made a call. He turned. He
was not her husband! Another man was in
her husband's clothes, a man with a villainous
countenance! With a scream she gave the
alarm. The stranger turned, dropped his
drink, bounded to the door and out, leaped to

the back of Beetle, gave rein and spur, and
the black horse made good his reputation.
In a second all was hue-and-cry and pursuit.
While men and horses made, for all they were
worth, down the road after Beetle, she on
Maid Marion galloped for her life in the opposite direction, the direction of the court town
whither her husband had journeyed. The
mare's hide made acquaintance with the whip
that day if never before, for not even the will-
ing Maid Marion could keep pace with the
apprehensions on her back.

Scouring with her eyes the highway ahead
of her, shooting hawk's glances into the forest
on each side of her, the wife rode through
the distance all, all day, praying that the day
might be long enough, might equal the distance. The sun set, and night began to fall;
but she and Maid Marion were none the less
fresh, except in the heart.

The moon rose straight before them down
the road, lighting it and them through the
threatened obscurity. And so they came to
trampled earth and torn grass, and so she un-
covered concealed footsteps, and so, creeping
on her hands and knees, she followed traces
of blood, through thicket and glade, into the

deep forest, to a hastily piled hillock of earth, gravel, and leaves. Burrowing with her hands, she came to it, the naked body of her young husband, cold and stiff, foully murdered.

Maid Marion approached at her call. She wrapped him in her cloak, and — a young wife of those times alone would do it — put him in the saddle before her : the good mare Maid Marion alone knows the rest. In the early gray dawn, from one highway there rode into the town the baffled pursuers, from the other the grandmother's grandmother, clasping the corpse of her husband with arms as stiff as his own ; loving him, so the grandmother used to say, with a love which, if ever love could do so, would have effected a resurrection.

THE OLD LADY'S RESTORATION

THE OLD LADY'S RESTORATION

THE news came out in the papers that the old lady had been restored to her fortune. She had been deprived of it so long ago that the real manner of her dispossession had become lost, or at least hidden under the many versions that had been invented to replace lapses of memory, or to remedy the unpicturesqueness of the original truth. The face of truth, like the face of many a good woman, is liable to the accident of ugliness, and the desire to embellish one as well as the other need not necessarily proceed from anything more harmful than an overweighted love of the beautiful.

If the old lady had not been restored to her fortune, her *personalia* would have remained in the oblivion which, as one might say, had accumulated upon everything belonging to her. But after that newspaper paragraph, there was such a flowering of

memory around her name as would have
done credit to a whole cemetery on All
Saints. It took three generations to do
justice to the old lady, for so long and so
slow had been her descent into poverty that
a grandmother was needed to remember her
setting out upon the road to it.

She set out as most people do, well provided with money, diamonds, pretty clothing,
handsome residence, equipage, opera-box,
beaus (for she was a widow), and so many,
many friends that she could never indulge
in a small party—she always had to give
a grand ball to accommodate them. She
made quite an occasion of her first reverse,—
some litigation decided against her,—and
said it came from the court's having only
one ear, and that preëmpted by the other
party.

She always said whatever she thought, re-
gardless of the consequences, because she
averred truth was so much more interesting
than falsehood. Nothing annoyed her more
in society than to have to listen to the com-
positions women make as a substitute for
the original truth. It was as if, when she
went to the theater to hear Shakspere and

Molière, the actors should try to impose upon
the audience by reciting lines of their own.
Truth was the wit of life and the wit of
books.   She traveled her road from affluence
so leisurely that nothing escaped her eyes
or her feelings, and she signaled unhesitatingly every stage in it.

"My dear, do you know there is really
such a thing as existence without a carriage
and horses?"—"I assure you it is perfectly
new to me to find that an opera-box is not
a necessity.   It is a luxury.   In theory one
can really never tell the distinction between
luxuries and necessities."—"How absurd!
At one time I thought hair was given us
only to furnish a profession to hair-dressers;
just as we wear artificial flowers to support
the flower-makers."—"Upon my word, it
is not uninteresting.   There is always some
haute nouveauté in economy.   The ways of
depriving one's self are infinite.   There is
wine, now."—"Not own your residence!
As soon not own your tomb as your residence!   My mama used to scream that in
my ears.   According to her, it was not
comme il faut to board or live in a rented
house.   How little she knew!"

When her friends, learning her increasing difficulties, which they did from the best authority (herself), complimented her, as they were forced to do, upon her still handsome appearance, pretty laces, feathers, jewelry, silks, "Fat," she would answer—"fat. I am living off my fat, as bears do in winter. In truth, I remind myself of an animal in more ways than one."

And so every one had something to contribute to the conversation about her—bits which, they said, affection and admiration had kept alive in their memory.

Each city has its own roads to certain ends, its ways of Calvary, so to speak. In New Orleans the victim seems ever to walk down Royal street and up Chartres, or *vice versa*. One would infer so, at least, from the display in the shops and windows of those thoroughfares. Old furniture, cut glass, pictures, books, jewelry, lace, china—the fleece (sometimes the flesh still sticking to it) left on the brambles by the driven herd. If there should some day be a trump of resurrection for defunct fortunes, those shops would be emptied in the same twinkling of the eye allowed to tombs for their rendition of property.

The old lady must have made that prome-
nade many, many times, to judge by the sam-
ples of her "fat or fleece" displayed in the
windows. She took to hobbling, as if from
tired or sore feet.

"It is nothing," in answer to an inquiry.
"Made-to-order feet learning to walk in
ready-made shoes : that is all. One's feet,
after all, are the most unintelligent part of
one's body." Tea was her abomination, coffee her adoration; but she explained: "Tea,
you know, is so detestable that the very
worst is hardly worse than the very best;
while coffee is so perfect that the smallest
shade of impurity is not to be tolerated. The
truly economical, I observe, always drink tea."
"At one time I thought if all the luxuries of
the world were exposed to me, and but one
choice allowed, I should select gloves. Believe me, there is no superfluity in the world
so easily dispensed with."

As may be supposed, her path led her
farther and farther away from her old friends.
Even her intimates became scarce; so much
so, that these observations, which, of course,
could be made only to intimates, became
fewer and fewer, unfortunately, for her cir-

12*

cumstances were becoming such that the
remarks became increasingly valuable. The
last thing related of her was apropos of
friends.

"My friends! My dear, I cannot tell you
just so, on the spur of the moment, but with
a little reflection and calculation I could tell
you, to a picayune, the rent of every friend
in the market. You can lease, rent, or hire
them, like horses, carriages, opera-boxes, servants, by year, month, day, or hour; and the
tariff is just as fixed.

"Christians! Christians are the most discreet people in the world. If you should ask
me what Christianity has most promoted in
the world, I should answer without hesitation,
discretion. Of course, when I say the world
I mean society, and when I say Christianity I
mean our interpretation of it. If only duns
could be pastors, and pastors duns! But of
course you do not know what duns are; they
are the guardian angels of the creditor, the
pursuing fiends of the debtor."

After that, the old lady made her disap-
pearance under the waves of that sea into the
depths of which it is very improbable that a
single friend ever attempted to pursue her.

And there she remained until the news came
that she was restored to fortune.

A week passed, two weeks; no sight or
sound of her.   It was during this period that
her old friends were so occupied resuscitating
their old friendships for her—when all her
antique sayings and doings became current
ball-room and dinner-table gossip—that she
arose from her obscurity like Cinderella from
her ashes, to be decked with every gift that
fairy minds could suggest.   Those who had
known her intimately made no effort to conceal their importance.   Those who did not
know her personally put forward claims of
inherited friendship, and those who did not
know her traditionally or otherwise—the
nouveaux riches and *parvenus*, who alone
feel the moneyed value of such social connec-
tions—began making their resolutions to
capture her as soon as she came in sight of
society.

The old residence was to be rebought, and
refurnished from France; the *avant scène* at
the opera had been engaged; the old cook
was to be hired back from the club at a fabu-
lous price; the old balls and the old dinners
were to gladden the city—so said they who

seemed to know.   Nothing was to be spared, nothing stinted—at her age, with no child or relative, and life running short for pleasure. Diamonds, laces, velvets, champagne, Château Yquem—" Grand Dieu Seigneur ! " the old Creole servants exclaimed, raising their hands at the enumeration of it.

Where the news came from nobody knew, but everything was certified and accepted as facts, although, as between women, the grain of salt should have been used.   Impatience waxed, until nearly every day some one would ring the bell of the old residence, to ask when the mistress was going to move in. And such affectionate messages ! And people would not, simply could not, be satisfied with the incomprehensible answers.   And then it leaked out.   The old lady was simply waiting for everything to arrive—furniture, toilets, carriage, etc.—to make a grand *entrée* into her old sphere; to come riding on a throne, as it were.   And still the time passed, and she did not come.   Finally two of the clever-heads penetrated the enigma : *mauvaise honte*, shyness—so long out of the world, so old; perhaps not sure of her welcome.   So they determined to seek her out.

THE ROOM IN THE OLD GALLERY.

"We will go to her, like children to a grandmother, etc.   The others have no delicacy of sentiment, etc.   And she will thus learn who really remember, really love her, etc."

Provided with congratulatory bouquets, they set forth.   It is very hard to find a dweller on the very sea-bottom of poverty. Perhaps that is why the effort is so seldom made.   One has to ask at grocers' shops, groggeries, market-stalls, Chinese restaurants; interview corner cobblers, ragpickers, gutter children.   But nothing is impossible to the determined.   The two ladies overcame all obstacles, and needled their way along, where under other circumstances they would not have glanced, would have thought it improper to glance.

They were directed through an old, old house, out on an old, old gallery, to a room at the very extreme end.

"Poor thing! Evidently she has not heard the good news yet.   We will be the first to communicate it," they whispered, standing before the dilapidated, withered-looking door.

Before knocking, they listened, as it is the very wisdom of discretion to do.   There was life inside, a little kind of voice, like some one trying to hum a song with a very cracked old throat.

The ladies opened the door. "Ah, my friend!"

"Ah, my friend!"

"Restored!"

"Restored!"

"At last!"

"At last!"

"Just the same!"

"Exactly the same!"

It was which one would get to her first with bouquet and kiss, competition almost crowding friendship.

"The good news!"

"The good news!"

"We could not stay!"

"We had to come!"

"It has arrived at last!"

"At last it has arrived!"

The old lady was very much older, but still the same.

"You will again have a chance!"

"Restored to your friends!"

"The world!"

"Your luxuries!"

" Your comforts ! "

" Comforts ! Luxuries ! " At last the old
lady had an opportunity to slip in a word.
" And friends ! You say right."

There was a pause—a pause which held
not a small measure of embarrassment. But
the two visitors, although they were women
of the world, and so dreaded an embarrassment more than they did sin, had prepared
themselves even to stand this.

The old lady standing there—she was very
much thinner, very much bent, but still the
same—appeared to be looking not at them,
but at their enumeration.

" Comfort ! " She opened a pot bubbling
on the fire. " Bouillon ! A good five-cent
bouillon. Luxury ! " She picked up something from a chair, a handful of new cotton
chemises. " Luxury ! " She turned back her
bedspread : new cotton sheets. "Did you
ever lie in your bed at night and dream of
sheets ? Comfort ! Luxury ! I should say so !
And friends ! My dear, look ! " Opening her
door, pointing to an opposite gallery, to the
yard, her own gallery ; to the washing, iron-
ing, sewing women, the cobbling, chair-
making, carpentering men ; to the screaming,

laughing, crying, quarreling, swarming children. "Friends! All friends—friends for
fifteen years. Ah, yes, indeed! We are all
glad—elated in fact. As you say. I am
restored."

The visitors simply reported that they had
found the old lady, and that she was imbecile;
mind completely gone under stress of poverty and old age. Their opinion was that
she should be interdicted.

A DELICATE AFFAIR

A DELICATE AFFAIR

"BUT what does this extraordinary display of light mean?" ejaculated my aunt, the moment she entered the parlor from the dining-room. "It looks like the kingdom of heaven in here! Jules! Jules!" she called, "come and put out some of the light!"

Jules was at the front door letting in the usual Wednesday-evening visitor, but now he came running in immediately with his own invention in the way of a gas-stick,—a piece of broom-handle notched at the end,—and began turning one tap after the other, until the room was reduced to complete darkness.

"But what do you mean now, Jules?" screamed the old lady again.

"Pardon, madame," answered Jules, with dignity; "it is an accident. I thought there was one still lighted."

"An accident! An accident! Do you think I hire you to perform accidents for me?

You are just through telling me that it was
accident made you give me both soup and
gumbo for dinner to-day."

"But accidents can always happen, madame," persisted Jules, adhering to his position.

The chandelier, a design of originality in its
day, gave light by what purported to be wax
candles standing each in a circlet of pendent
crystals. The usual smile of ecstatic admiration spread over Jules's features as he
touched the match to the simulated wicks,
and lighted into life the rainbows in the prisms
underneath. It was a smile that did not heighten the intelligence of his features, revealing
as it did the toothless condition of his gums.

"What will madame have for her dinner
to-morrow," looking benignantly at his mistress, and still standing under his aureole.

"Do I ever give orders for one dinner,
with the other one still on my lips?"

"I only asked madame; there is no harm
in asking." He walked away, his long stiff
white apron rattling like a petticoat about
him. Catching sight of the visitor still standing at the threshold: "Oh, madame, here is
Mr. Horace. Shall I let him in?"

"Idiot! Every Wednesday you ask me that question, and every Wednesday I answer the same way. Don't you think I could tell you when not to let him in without your asking?"

"Oh, well, madame, one never knows; it is always safe to ask."

The appearance of the gentleman started a fresh subject of excitement.

"Jules! Jules! You have left that front door unlocked again!"

"Excuse me," said Mr. Horace; "Jules did not leave the front door unlocked. It was locked when I rang, and he locked it again most carefully after letting me in. I have been standing outside all the while the gas was being extinguished and relighted."

"Ah, very well, then. And what is the news?" She sank into her arm-chair, pulled her little card-table closer, and began shuffling the cards upon it for her game of solitaire. "I never hear any news, you know. She [nodding toward me] goes out, but she never learns anything. She is as stupid to-night as an empty bottle."

After a few passes her hands, which were slightly tremulous, regained some of their

wonted steadiness and brilliancy of movement, and the cards dropped rapidly on the
table.   Mr. Horace, as he had got into the
habit of doing, watched her mechanically,
rather absent-mindedly retailing what he
imagined would interest her, from his week's
observation and hearsay.   And madame's
little world revolved, complete for her, in
time, place, and personality.

It was an old-fashioned square room with
long ceiling, and broad, low windows heavily
curtained with stiff silk brocade, faded by
time into mellowness.   The tall white-painted
mantel carried its obligation of ornaments
well : a gilt clock which under a glass case
related some brilliant poetical idyl, and told
the hours only in an insignificant aside, according to the delicate politeness of bygone
French taste ; flanked by duplicate continua-
tions of the same idyl in companion cande-
labra, also under glass ; Sèvres, or imitation
Sèvres vases, and a crowd of smaller objects
to which age and rarity were slowly contributing an artistic value.   An oval mirror
behind threw replicas of them into another
mirror, receiving in exchange the reflected
portrait of madame in her youth, and in the

partial nudity in which innocence was limned
in madame's youth. There were besides
mirrors on the other three walls of the room,
all hung with such careful intent for the exercise of their vocation that the apartment,
in spots, extended indefinitely; the brilliant
chandelier was thereby quadrupled, and the
furniture and ornaments multiplied everywhere and most unexpectedly into twins and
triplets, producing such sociabilities among
them, and forcing such correspondences between inanimate objects with such hospitable
insistence, that the effect was full of gaiety
and life, although the interchange in reality
was the mere repetition of one original, a
kind of phonographic echo.

The portrait of monsieur, madame's handsome young husband, hung out of the circle
of radiance, in the isolation that, wherever
they hang, always seems to surround the
portraits of the dead.

Old as the parlors appeared, madame ante-
dated them by the sixteen years she had
lived before her marriage, which had been
the occasion of their furnishment. She had
traveled a considerable distance over the
sands of time since the epoch commemorated

13*

by the portrait. Indeed, it would require almost documentary evidence to prove that she, who now was arriving at eighty, was the same Atalanta that had started out so buoyantly at sixteen.

Instead of a cap, she wore black lace over her head, pinned with gold brooches. Her white hair curled naturally over a low forehead. Her complexion showed care—and powder. Her eyes were still bright, not with the effete intelligence of old age, but with actual potency. She wore a loose black sack flowered in purple, and over that a black lace mantle, fastened with more gold brooches.

She played her game of solitaire rapidly, impatiently, and always won; for she never hesitated to cheat to get out of a tight place, or into a favorable one, cheating with the quickness of a flash, and forgetting it the moment afterward.

Mr. Horace was as old as she, but he looked much younger, although his dress and appearance betrayed no evidence of an effort in that direction. Whenever his friend cheated, he would invariably call her attention to it; and as usual she would shrug her shoulders, and say, "Bah! lose a game for a card!" and pursue the conversation.

He happened to mention mushrooms— fresh mushrooms. She threw down her cards before the words were out of his mouth, and began to call, "Jules! Jules!" Mr. Horace pulled the bell-cord, but madame was too excitable for that means of communication. She ran into the antechamber, and put her head over the banisters, calling, "Jules! Jules!" louder and louder. She might have heard Jules's slippered feet running from the street into the corridor and up-stairs, had she not been so deaf. He appeared at the door.

"But where have you been? Here I have been raising the house a half-hour, calling you. You have been in the street. I am sure you have been in the street."

"Madame is very much mistaken," answered Jules, with resentful dignity. He had taken off his white apron of waiter, and was disreputable in all the shabbiness of his attire as cook. "When madame forbids me to go into the street, I do not go into the street. I was in the kitchen; I had fallen asleep. What does madame desire?" smiling benevolently.

"What is this I hear? Fresh mushrooms in the market!"

"Eh, madame?"

"Fresh mushrooms in the market, and you have not brought me any!"

"Madame, there are fresh mushrooms everywhere in the market," waving his hand to show their universality.

"Everybody is eating them —"

"Old Pomponnette," Jules continued, "only this morning offered me a plate, piled up high, for ten cents."

"Idiot! Why did you not buy them?"

"If madame had said so; but madame did not say so. Madame said, 'Soup, Jules; carrots, rice,'" counting on his fingers.

"And the gumbo?"

"I have explained that that was an accident. Madame said 'Soup,'" enumerating his menu again; "madame never once said mushrooms."

"But how could I know there were mushrooms in the market? Do I go to market?"

"That is it!" and Jules smiled at the question thus settled.

"If you had told me there were mushrooms in the market—" pursued madame, persisting in treating Jules as a reasonable being.

"Why did not madame ask me? If
madame had asked me, surely I would have
told madame. Yesterday Cæsar brought
them to the door—a whole bucketful for
twenty-five cents. I had to shut the door in
his face to get rid of him," triumphantly.

"And you brought me yesterday those
detestable peas!"

"Ah," shrugging his shoulders, "madame
told me to buy what I saw. I saw peas. I
bought them."

"Well, understand now, once for all: whenever you see mushrooms, no matter what I
ordered, you buy them. Do you hear?"

"No, madame. Surely I cannot buy mushrooms unless madame orders them. Madame's
disposition is too quick."

"But I do order them. Stupid! I do order
them. I tell you to buy them every day."

"And if there are none in the market
every day?"

"Go away! Get out of my sight! I do not
want to see you. Ah, it is unendurable! I
must—I must get rid of him!" This last was
not a threat, as Jules knew only too well. It
was merely a habitual exclamation.

During the colloquy Mr. Horace, leaning
back in his arm-chair, raised his eyes, and

caught the reflected portrait of madame in
the mirror before him — the reflection so
much softer and prettier, so much more
ethereal, than the original painting. Indeed,
seen in the mirror, that way, the portrait was
as refreshing as the most charming memory.
He pointed to it when madame, with considerable loss of temper, regained her seat.

"It is as beautiful as the past," he explained most unnaturally, for he and his
friend had a horror of looking at the long,
long past, which could not fail to remind
them of — what no one cares to contemplate
out of church. Making an effort toward
some determination which a subtle observer
might have noticed weighing upon him all
the evening, he added: "And, apropos of
the past — "

"*Hein?*" interrogated the old lady, impatiently, still under the influence of her irasci-
bility about the mushrooms.

He moved his chair closer, and bent forward, as if his communication were to be
confidential.

"Ah, bah! Speak louder!" she cried.
"One would suppose you had some secret to
tell. What secrets can there be at our age?"

She took up her cards and began to play.
There could be no one who bothered herself
less about the forms of politeness.

"Yes, yes," answered Mr. Horace, throwing himself back into his chair; "what secrets can there be at our age?"

The remark seemed a pregnant one to
him; he gave himself up to it. One must
evidently be the age of one's thoughts. Mr.
Horace's thoughts revealed him the old man
he was. The lines in his face deepened into
wrinkles; his white mustache could not pre-
tend to conceal his mouth, worsened by the
loss of a tooth or two; and the long, thin
hand that propped his head was crossed with
blue, distended veins. "At the last judgment"—it was a favorite quotation with him
—"the book of our conscience will be read
aloud before the whole company."

But the old lady, deep in her game, paid
no more heed to his quotation than to him.
He made a gesture toward her portrait.

"When that was painted, Josephine—"

Madame threw a glance after the gesture.
The time was so long ago, the mythology of
Greece hardly more distant! At eighty
the golden age of youth must indeed appear

an evanescent myth.   Madame's ideas seemed
to take that direction.

"Ah, at that time we were all nymphs,
and you all demigods."

"Demigods and nymphs, yes; but there
was one among us who was a god with
you all."

The allusion—a frequent one with Mr.
Horace—was to madame's husband, who in
his day, it is said, had indeed played the god
in the little Arcadia of society.   She shrugged
her shoulders.   The truth is so little of a
compliment.   The old gentleman sighed in
an abstracted way, and madame, although
apparently absorbed in her game, lent her
ear.   It is safe to say that a woman is
never too old to hear a sigh wafted in her
direction.

"Josephine, do you remember—in your
memory—"

She pretended not to hear.   Remember?
Who ever heard of her forgetting?   But she
was not the woman to say, at a moment's
notice, what she remembered or what she
forgot.

"A woman's memory!   When I think of
a woman's memory—in fact, I do not like to

think of a woman's memory. One can in-
trude in imagination into many places; but a
woman's memory—"

Mr. Horace seemed to lose his thread. It
had been said of him in his youth that he
wrote poetry—and it was said against him.
It was evidently such lapses as these that
had given rise to the accusation. And as
there was no one less impatient under sentiment or poetry than madame, her feet began
to agitate themselves as if Jules were perora-
ting some of his culinary inanities before her.

"And a man's memory!" totally misunder-
standing him. "It is not there that I either
would penetrate, my friend. A man—"

When madame began to talk about men
she was prompted by imagination just as
much as was Mr. Horace when he talked
about women. But what a difference in their
sentiments! And yet he had received so
little, and she so much, from the subjects of
their inspiration. But that seems to be the
way in life — or in imagination.

"That you should" — he paused with the
curious shyness of the old before the word
"love" — "that you two should — marry —
seemed natural, inevitable, at the time."

Tradition records exactly the same comment by society at the time on the marriage in question.   Society is ever fatalistic in its comments.

"But the natural — the inevitable — do we not sometimes, I wonder, perform them as Jules does his accidents?"

"Ah, do not talk about that idiot! An idiot born and bred! I won't have him about me! He is a monstrosity! I tell his grandmother that every day when she comes to comb me. What a farce — what a ridiculous farce comfortable existence has become with us! Fresh mushrooms in market, and bring me carrots!"

The old gentleman, partly from long knowledge of her habit, or from an equally persistent bend of his own, quietly held on to his idea.

"One cannot tell. It seems so at the time. We like to think it so; it makes it easier. And yet, looking back on our future as we once looked forward to it — "

"Eh! but who wants to look back on it, my friend? Who in the world wants to look back on it?" One could not doubt madame's energy of opinion on that question to hear her voice. "We have done our future, we have performed it, if you will. Our future! It is like the dinners we have eaten; of course we cannot remember the good without becoming exasperated over the bad: but—" shrugging her shoulders—"since we cannot beat the cooks, we must submit to fate," forcing a queen that she needed at the critical point of her game.

"At sixteen and twenty-one it is hard to realize that one is arranging one's life to last until sixty, seventy, forever," correcting himself as he thought of his friend, the dead husband. If madame had ever possessed the art of self-control, it was many a long day since she had exercised it; now she frankly began to show ennui.

"When I look back to that time,"—Mr. Horace leaned back in his chair and half closed his eyes, perhaps to avoid the expression of her face,—"I see nothing but lights and flowers, I hear nothing but music and laughter; and all—lights and flowers and music and laughter—seem to meet in this room, where we met so often to arrange our —inevitabilities." The word appeared to attract him. "Josephine,"—with a sudden change of voice and manner,—"Josephine, how beautiful you were!"

The old lady nodded her head without looking from her cards.

"They used to say," with sad conviction of the truth of his testimony—"the men used to say that your beauty was irresistible. None ever withstood you. None ever could."

That, after all, was Mr. Horace's great charm with madame; he was so faithful to the illusions of his youth. As he looked now at her, one could almost feel the irresistibility of which he spoke.

"It was only their excuse, perhaps; we could not tell at the time; we cannot tell even now when we think about it. They said then, talking as men talk over such things, that you were the only one who could remain yourself under the circumstances; you were the only one who could know, who could will, under the circumstances. It was their theory; men can have only theories about such things." His voice dropped, and he seemed to drop too, into some abysm of thought.

Madame looked into the mirror, where she could see the face of the one who alone could

retain her presence of mind under the circumstances suggested by Mr. Horace. She
could also have seen, had she wished it,
among the reflected bric-a-brac of the mantel, the corner of the frame that held the
picture of her husband, but peradventure,
classing it with the past which held so many
unavenged bad dinners, she never thought to
link it even by a look with her emotions of
the present. Indeed, it had been said of her
that in past, present, and future there had
ever been but the one picture to interest her
eyes—the one she was looking at now.
This, however, was the remark of the uni-
nitiated, for the true passion of a beautiful
woman is never so much for her beauty as
for its booty; as the passion of a gamester is
for his game, not for his luck.

"How beautiful *she* was!"

It was apparently down in the depths of
his abysm that he found the connection between this phrase and his last, and it was
evidently to himself he said it. Madame,
however, heard and understood too; in fact,
traced back to a certain period, her thoughts
and Mr. Horace's must have been fed by
pretty much the same subjects. But she had

14

so carefully barricaded certain issues in her
memory as almost to obstruct their flow into
her life; if she were a cook, one would say
that it was her bad dinners which she was
trying to keep out of remembrance.

"You there, he there, she there, I there."
He pointed to the places on the carpet, under
the chandelier; he could have touched them
with a walking-stick, and the recollection
seemed just as close.

"She was, in truth, what we men called
her then; it was her eyes that first suggested
it—Myosotis, the little blue flower, the for-
get-me-not. It suited her better than her
own name. We always called her that
among ourselves. How beautiful she was!"
He leaned his head on his hand and looked
where he had seen her last—so long, such
an eternity, ago.

It must be explained for the benefit of
those who do not live in the little world where
an allusion is all that is necessary to put one
in full possession of any drama, domestic or
social, that Mr. Horace was speaking of the
wedding-night of madame, when the bridal
party stood as he described under the chandelier; the bride and groom, with each one's

best friend. It may be said that it was the
last night or time that madame had a best
friend of her own sex. Social gossip, with
characteristic kindness, had furnished reasons
to suit all tastes, why madame had ceased
that night to have a best friend of her own
sex. If gossip had not done so, society would
still be left to its imagination for information,
for madame never tolerated the smallest ap-
peal to her for enlightenment. What the
general taste seemed most to relish as a ver-
sion was that madame in her marriage had
triumphed, not conquered; and that the night
of her wedding she had realized the fact, and,
to be frank, had realized it ever since. In short,
madame had played then to gain at love, as
she played now to gain at solitaire; and
hearts were no more than cards to her—and,
"Bah! Lose a game for a card!" must have
been always her motto. It is hard to explain
it delicately enough, for these are the most
delicate affairs in life; but the image of Myosotis had passed through monsieur's heart,
and Myosotis does mean "forget me not."
And madame well knew that to love monsieur
once was to love him always, in spite of jeal-
ousy, doubt, distrust, nay, unhappiness (for to

love him meant all this and more).   He was
that kind of man, they said, whom women
could love even against conscience.   Madame never forgave that moment.   Her
friend, at least, she could put aside out of her
intercourse; unfortunately, we cannot put
people out of our lives.   God alone can do
that, and so far he had interfered in the matter only by removing monsieur.   It was
known to notoriety that since her wedding
madame had abandoned, destroyed, all knowledge of her friend.   And the friend?   She
had disappeared as much as is possible for
one in her position and with her duties.

   "What there is in blue eyes, light hair, and
a fragile form to impress one, I cannot tell;
but for us men it seems to me it is blue-eyed,
light-haired, and fragile-formed women that
are the hardest to forget."

   "The less easy to forget," corrected
madame; but he paid no attention to the
remark.

   "They are the women that attach themselves in one's memory.   If necessary to
keep from being forgotten, they come back
into one's dreams.   And as life rolls on, one
wonders about them,—'Is she happy? Is

she miserable? Goes life well or ill with
her?'"

Madame played her cards slowly, one
would say, for her, prosaically.

"And there is always a pang when, as one
is so wondering, the response comes,—that
is, the certainty in one's heart responds,—
'She is miserable, and life goes ill with
her.' Then, if ever, men envy the power
of God."

Madame threw over the game she was in,
and began a new one.

"Such women should not be unhappy;
they are too fragile, too sensitive, too trusting. I could never understand the infliction
of misery upon them. I could send death to
them, but not—not misfortune."

Madame, forgetting again to cheat in time,
and losing her game, began impatiently to
shuffle her cards for a new deal.

"And yet, do you know, Josephine, those
women are the unhappy ones of life. They
seem predestined to it, as others"—looking
at madame's full-charmed portrait—"are
predestined to triumph and victory. They"
—unconscious, in his abstraction, of the personal nature of his simile—"never know

14*

how to handle their cards, and they always
play a losing game."

"Ha!" came from madame, startled into
an irate ejaculation.

"It is their love always that is sacrificed,
their hearts always that are bruised. One
might say that God himself favors the black-
haired ones!"

As his voice sank lower and lower, the
room seemed to become stiller and stiller.
A passing vehicle in the street, however, now
and then drew a shiver of sound from the
pendent prisms of the chandelier.

"She was so slight, so fragile, and always
in white, with blue in her hair to match her
eyes—and—God knows what in her heart,
all the time. And yet they stand it, they
bear it, they do not die, they live along with
the strongest, the happiest, the most fortu-
nate of us," bitterly; "and"—raising his eyes
to his old friend, who thereupon immediately
began to fumble her cards —"whenever in
the street I see a poor, bent, broken woman's
figure, I know, without verifying it any more
by a glance, that it is the wreck of a fair
woman's figure; whenever I hear of a bent,
broken existence, I know, without asking

any more, that it is the wreck of a fair
woman's life."

Poor Mr. Horace spoke with the unrea-
son of a superstitious bigot.

"I have often thought, since, in large
assemblies, particularly in weddings, Josephine, of what was going on in the women's
hearts there, and I have felt sorry for them;
and when I think of God's knowing what
is in their hearts, I have felt sorry for the
men. And I often think now, Josephine,—
I think oftener and oftener of it,—that if the
resurrection trumpet of our childhood should
sound some day, no matter when, out there,
over the old St. Louis cemetery, and we
should all have to rise from our long rest
of oblivion, what would be the first thing
we should do? And though there were a
God and a heaven awaiting us,—by that
same God, Josephine, I believe that our
first thought in awakening would be the
last in dying,—confession,—and that our
first rush would be to the feet of one another for forgiveness. For there are some
offenses that must outlast the longest oblivion, and a forgiveness that will be more
necessary than God's own. Then our hearts

will be bared to one another; for if, as
you say, there are no secrets at our age,
there can still be less cause for them after
death."

His voice ended in the faintest whisper.
The table crashed over, and the cards flew
wide-spread on the floor.   Before we could
recover, madame was in the antechamber,
screaming for Jules.

One would have said that, from her face,
the old lady had witnessed the resurrection
described by Mr. Horace, the rush of the
spirits with their burdens of remorse, the one
to the feet of the other; and she must have
seen herself and her husband, with a una-
nimity of purpose never apparent in their
short married life, rising from their common
tomb and hastening to that other tomb at the
end of the alley, and falling at the feet of the
one to whom in life he had been recreant in
love, she in friendship.

Of course Jules answered through the
wrong door, rushing in with his gas-stick, and
turning off the gas.   In a moment we were
involved in darkness and dispute.

" But what does he mean ?   What does the
idiot mean?   He—"   It was impossible for

her to find a word to do justice to him and to her exasperation at the same time.

"Pardon, madame; it is not I. It is the cathedral bell; it is ringing nine o'clock."

"But—"

"Madame can hear it herself. Listen!" We could not see it, but we were conscious of the benign, toothless smile spreading over his face as the bell-tones fell in the room.

"But it is not the gas. I—"

"Pardon, madame; but it is the gas. Madame said, 'Jules, put out the gas every night when the bell rings.' Madame told me that only last night. The bell rings: I put out the gas."

"Will you be silent? Will you listen?"

"If madame wishes; just as madame says."

But the old lady had turned to Mr. Horace. "Horace, you have seen—you know—" and it was a question now of overcoming emotion. "I—I—I—a carriage, my friend, a carriage."

"Madame—" Jules interrupted his smile to interrupt her.

She was walking around the room, picking up a shawl here, a lace there; for she was always prepared against draughts.

" Madame — " continued Jules, pursuing her.

" A carriage."

" If madame would only listen, I was going to say — but madame is too quick in her disposition — the carriage has been waiting since a long hour ago. Mr. Horace said to have it there in a half hour."

It was then she saw for the first time that it had all been prepared by Mr. Horace. The rest was easy enough: getting into the carriage, and finding the place of which Mr. Horace had heard, as he said, only that afternoon. In it, on her bed of illness, poverty, and suffering, lay the patient, wasted form of the beautiful fair one whom men had called in her youth Myosotis.

But she did not call her Myosotis.

" *Mon Amour !* " The old pet name, although it had to be fetched across more than half a century of disuse, flashed like lightning from madame's heart into the dim chamber.

" *Ma Divine !* " came in counter-flash from the curtained bed.

In the old days women, or at least young girls, could hazard such pet names one upon the other. These — think of it! — dated from

the first communion class, the dating period
of so much of friendship.

" My poor Amour !"

" My poor, poor Divine !"

The voices were together, close beside the
pillow.

"I—I—" began Divine.

"It could not have happened if God had
not wished it," interrupted poor Amour, with
the resignation that comes, alas! only with
the last drop of the bitter cup.

And that was about all. If Mr. Horace
had not slipped away, he might have noticed
the curious absence of monsieur's name, and
of his own name, in the murmuring that followed. It would have given him some more
ideas on the subject of woman.

At any rate, the good God must thank him
for having one affair the less to arrange when
the trumpet sounds out there over the old St.
Louis cemetery. And he was none too pre-
mature; for the old St. Louis cemetery, as
was shortly enough proved, was a near reach
for all three of the old friends.

A DELICATE AFFAIR

PUPASSE

PUPASSE

EVERY day, every day, it was the same overture in Madame Joubert's room in the Institut St. Denis; the strident:

"Mesdemoiselles; à vos places! Notre Père qui est dans le ciel—Qui a fait ce bruit?"

"It's Pupasse, madame! It's Pupasse!" The answer invariably was unanimous.

"But, Madame Joubert,—I assure you, Madame Joubert,—I could not help it! They know I could not help it!"

By this time the fresh new fool's cap made from yesterday's "Bee" would have been pinned on her head.

"Quelle injustice! Quelle injustice!"

This last apostrophe in a high, whining nasal voice, always procured Pupasse's elevation on the tall three-legged stool in the corner.

It was a theory of the little girls in the primary class that Madame Joubert would be

much more lenient to their own little inevitabilities of bad conduct and lessons if Pupasse did not invariably comb her the wrong
way every morning after prayers, by dropping
something, or sniffling, or sneezing. There-
fore, while they distractedly got together
books, slates, and copy-books, their infantile
eyes found time to dart deadly reproaches
toward the corner of penitence, and their little lips, still shaped from their first nourishment, pouted anything but sympathy for the
occupant of it.

Indeed, it would have been a most startling
unreality to have ever entered Madame Joubert's room and not seen Pupasse in that corner, on that stool, her tall figure shooting up
like a post, until her tall, pointed *bonnet d' âne*
came within an inch or two of the ceiling. It
was her hoop-skirt that best testified to her
height. It was the period of those funnel-
shaped hoop-skirts that spread out with such
nice mathematical proportions, from the waist
down, that it seemed they must have ema-
nated from the brains of astronomers, like the
orbits, and diameters, and other things belonging to the heavenly bodies. Pupasse could
not have come within three feet of the wall

with her hoop-skirt distended. To have forced matters was not to be thought of an instant. So even in her greatest grief and indignation, she had to pause before the three-legged black stool, and gather up steel after steel of her circumference in her hands behind, until her calico skirt careened and flattened; and so she could manage to accommodate herself to the limited space of her punishment, the circles drooping far over her feet as she stood there, looking like the costumed stick of a baby's rattle.

Her thinness continued into her face, which, unfortunately, had nothing in the way of toilet to assist it. Two little black eyes fixed in the sides of a mere fence of a nose, and a mouth with the shape and expression of all mouths made to go over sharp-pointed teeth planted very far apart; the smallest amount possible of fine, dry, black hair—a perfect rat-tail when it was plaited in one, as almost all wore their hair. But sometimes Pupasse took it into her head to plait it in two braids, as none but the thick-haired ventured to wear it. As the little girls said, it was a petition to Heaven for "eau Quinquina." When Marcelite, the hair-dresser, came at

15

her regular periods to visit the hair of the
boarders, she would make an effort with
Pupasse, plaiting her hundred hairs in a ten-
strand braid. The effect was a half yard of
black worsted galloon; nothing more, or better. Had Pupasse possessed as many heads
as the hydra, she could have "coiffe'd"
them all with fools' caps during one morning's recitations. She entirely monopolized
the "Daily Bee." Madame Joubert was
forced to borrow from "madame" the stale
weekly "Courrier des Etats-Unis" for the
rest of the room. From grammar, through
sacred history, arithmetic, geography, mythology, down to dictation, Pupasse could pile
up an accumulation of penitences that would
have tasked the limits of the current day had
not recreation been wisely set as a term
which disbarred, by proscription, previous
offenses. But even after recreation, with that
day's lessons safely out, punished and expi-
ated, Pupasse's doom seemed scarcely light-
ened; there was still a whole criminal code of
conduct to infract. The only difference was
that instead of books, slates, or copy-books,
leathern medals, bearing various legends and
mottos, were hung around her neck — a tra-

vestied decoration worse than the books for
humiliation.

The "abécédaires," their torment for the
day over, thankful for any distraction from
the next day's lessons, and eager for any
relief from the intolerable ennui of goodness,
were thankful enough now for Pupasse.
They naturally watched her in preference to
Madame Joubert, holding their books and
slates quite cunningly to hide their faces.
Pupasse had not only the genius, but that
which sometimes fails genius, the means for
grimacing: little eyes, long nose, foolish
mouth, and pointed tongue. And she was
so amusing, when Madame Joubert's head
was turned, that the little girls, being young
and innocent, would forget themselves and
all burst out laughing. It sounded like a
flight of singing birds through the hot, close,
stupid little room; but not so to Madame
Joubert.

"Young ladies! But what does this
mean?"

And, terror-stricken, the innocents would
call out with one voice, "It's Pupasse, madame! It's Pupasse who made us laugh!"
There was nothing but fools' caps to be

gained by prevaricating, and there was fre-
quently nothing less gained by confession.
And oh, the wails and the sobs as the innocents would be stood up, one by one, in their
places! Even the pigtails at the backs of
their little heads were convulsed with grief.
Oh, how they hated Pupasse then! When
their *bonnes* came for them at three o'clock,—
washing their tear-stained faces at the cistern
before daring to take them through the
streets,—how passionately they would cry
out, the tears breaking afresh into the wet
handkerchiefs:

"It 's that Pupasse! It 's that *vilaine*
Pupasse!"

To Pupasse herself would be meted out
that "peine forte et dure," that acme of humiliation and disgrace, so intensely horrible
that many a little girl in that room solemnly
averred and believed she would kill herself
before submitting to it. Pupasse's volumi-
nous calico skirt would be gathered up by the
hem and tied up over her head! Oh, the
horrible monstrosity on the stool in the corner
then! There were no eyes in that room that
had any desire to look upon it. And the cries
and the "Quelle injustice!" that fell on the

ears then from the hidden feelings had all the
weirdness of the unseen, but heard.   And all
the other girls in the room, in fear and trem-
bling, would begin to move their lips in a
perfect whirlwind of study, or write violently
on their slates, or begin at that very instant to
rule off their copy-books for the next day's
verb.

Pupasse—her name was Marie Pupasse,
but no one thought of calling her anything
but Pupasse, with emphasis on the first sylla-
ble and sibilance on the last—had no parents,
only a grandmother, to describe whom, all
that is necessary to say is that she was as
short as Pupasse was tall, and that her face
resembled nothing so much as a little yellow
apple shriveling from decay.   The old lady
came but once a week, to fetch Pupasse fresh
clothes, and a great brown paper bag of nice
things to eat.   There was no boarder in the
school who received handsomer bags of cake
and fruit than Pupasse.   And although, not
two hours before, a girl might have been foremost in the shrill cry, " It is Pupasse who
made the noise! It is Pupasse who made me
laugh!" there was nothing in that paper bag
reserved even from such a one.   When the

15*

girl herself with native delicacy would, under the circumstances, judge it discreet to refuse, Pupasse would plead, "Oh, but take it to give me pleasure!" And if still the refusal continued, Pupasse would take her bag and go into the summer-house in the corner of the garden, and cry until the unforgiving one would relent. But the first offering of the bag was invariably to the stern dispenser of fools' caps and the unnamed humiliation of the reversed skirt: Madame Joubert.

Pupasse was in the fifth class. The sixth —the abécédaires—was the lowest in the school. Green was the color of the fifth; white—innocence—of the abécédaires. Exhibition after exhibition, the same green sash and green ribbons appeared on Pupasse's white muslin, the white muslin getting longer and longer every year, trying to keep up with her phenomenal growth; and always, from all over the room, buzzed the audience's suppressed merriment at Pupasse's appearance in the ranks of the little ones of nine and ten. It was that very merriment that brought about the greatest change in the Institut St. Denis. The sitting order of the classes was reversed. The first class—the graduates—

went up to the top step of the *estrade;* and
the little ones put on the lowest, behind the
pianos. The graduates grumbled that it was
not *comme il faut* to have young ladies of
their position stepping like camels up and
down those great steps; and the little girls
said it was a shame to hide them behind the
pianos after their mamas had taken so much
pains to make them look pretty. But madame said—going also to natural history for
her comparison—that one must be a rhinoce-
ros to continue the former routine.

Religion cannot be kept waiting forever on
the intelligence. It was always in the fourth
class that the first communion was made;
that is, when the girls stayed one year in
each class. But Pupasse had spent three
years in the sixth class, and had already been
four in the fifth, and Madame Joubert felt
that longer delay would be disrespectful to
the good Lord. It was true that Pupasse
could not yet distinguish the ten command-
ments from the seven capital sins, and still
would answer that Jeanne d'Arc was the
foundress of the "Little Sisters of the Poor."
But, as Madame Joubert always said in the
little address she made to the catechism class

every year before handing it over to Father
Dolomier, God judged from the heart, and
not from the mind.

Father Dolomier — from his face he would
have been an able contestant of *bonnets d'âne*
with Pupasse, if subjected to Madame Joubert's discipline — evidently had the same
method of judging as God, although the
catechism class said they could dance a
waltz on the end of his long nose without
his perceiving it.

There is always a little air of mystery
about the first communion : not that there is
any in reality, but the little ones assume it to
render themselves important. The going to
early mass, the holding their dog-eared catechisms as if they were relics, the instruction
from the priest, even if he were only old
Father Dolomier — it all put such a little air
of devotion into their faces that it imposed
(as it did every year) upon their companions,
which was a vastly gratifying effect. No
matter how young and innocent she may be,
a woman's devotion always seems to have
two aims — God and her own sex.

The week of retreat came. Oh, the week
of retreat ! That was the *bonne bouche* of it

all, for themselves and for the others. It was
the same every year. By the time the week
of retreat arrived, interest and mystery had
been frothed to the point of indiscretion; so
that the little girls would stand on tiptoe to
peep through the shutters at the postulants
inside, and even the larger girls, to whom
first communion was a thing of an infantile
past, would condescend to listen to their re-
ports with ill-feigned indifference.

As the day of the first communion neared,
the day of the general confession naturally
neared too, leading it. And then the little
girls, peeping through the shutters, and holding their breath to see better, saw what they
beheld every year; but it was always new
and awesome — mysterious scribbling in corners with lead-pencils on scraps of paper;
consultations; rewritings; copyings; the list
of their sins, of all the sins of their lives.

"*Ma chère!*"— pigtails and sunbonnets
hiving outside would shudder. "Oh, *Mon
Dieu!* To have to confess all—but *all* your
sins! As for me, it would kill me, sure!"

And the frightful recoils of their con-
sciences would make all instantly blanch and
cross themselves.

"And look at Pupasse's sins! Oh, but they are long! *Ma chère*, but look! But look, I ask you, at them!"

The longest record was of course the most complimentary and honorable to the possessor, as each girl naturally worked not only for absolution but for fame.

Between catechisms and instructions Madame Joubert would have "La Vie des Saints" read aloud, to stimulate their piety and to engage their thoughts; for the thoughts of first communicants are worse than flies for buzzing around the forbidden. The lecture must have been a great quickener of conscience; for they would dare punishment and cheat Madame Joubert, under her own eyes, in order surreptitiously to add a new sin to their list. Of course the one hour's recreation could not afford time enough for observation now, and the little girls were driven to all sorts of excuses to get out of the classroom for one moment's peep through the shutters; at which whole swarms of them would sometimes be caught and sent into punishment.

Only two days more. Madame Joubert put them through the rehearsal, a most im-

portant part of the preparation, almost as
important as catechism—how to enter the
church, how to hold the candle, how to advance, how to kneel, retire—everything, in
fact.

Only one day more, the quietest, most de-
votional day of all. Pupasse lost her sins!

Of course every year the same accident
happened to some one. But it was a new
accident to Pupasse. And such a long list!

The commotion inside that retreat! Pupasse's nasal whine, carrying her lament
without any mystery to the outside garden.
Such searching of pockets, rummaging of
corners, microscopic examination of the
floor! Such crimination and recrimination,
protestation, asseveration, assurances, backed
by divine and saintly invocations! Pupasse
accused companion after companion of filch-
ing her sins, which each after each would
violently deny, producing each her own list
from her own pocket,—proof to conviction of
innocence, and, we may say, of guilt also.

Pupasse declared they had filched it to
copy, because her list was the longest and
most complete. She could not go to confession without her sins; she could not go to

communion without confession. The tears rolled down her long thin nose unchecked, for she never could remember to use her handkerchief until reminded by Madame Joubert.

She had committed it to memory, as all the others had done theirs; but how was she to know without the list if she had not forgotten something? And to forget one thing in a general confession they knew was a mortal sin.

"I shall tell Madame Joubert! I shall tell Madame Joubert!"

"*Ma chère!*" whispered the little ones outside. "Oh, but look at them! *Elles font les quatre cents coups!*" which is equivalent to "cutting up like the mischief."

And with reason. As if such an influx of the world upon them at this moment were not sufficient of itself to damn them. But to tell Madame Joubert! With all their dresses made and ready, wreaths, veils, candles, prayer-books, picture-cards, mother-of-pearl prayer-beads, and festival breakfasts with admiring family and friends prepared. Tell Madame Joubert! She would simply cancel it all. In a body they chorused:

"But, Pupasse!"

" *Chère* Pupasse!"

" *Voyons*, Pupasse!"

"I assure you, Pupasse!"

"On the cross, Pupasse!"

" Ah, Pupasse!"

"We implore you, Pupasse!"

The only response—tears, and "I shall tell Madame Joubert."

Consultations, caucuses, individual appeals, general outbursts. Pupasse stood in the corner. Curiously, she always sought refuge in the very sanctum of punishment, her face hidden in her bended arms, her hoops standing out behind, vouchsafing nothing but tears, and the promise to tell Madame Joubert. And three o'clock approaching! And Madame Joubert imminent! But Pupasse really could not go to confession without her sins. They all recognized that; they were reasonable, as they assured her.

A crisis quickens the wits. They heard the cathedral clock strike the quarter to three. They whispered, suggested, argued—bunched in the farthest corner from Pupasse.

"Console yourself, Pupasse! We will help you, Pupasse! Say no more about it! We will help you!"

A delegate was sent to say that. She was only four feet and a half high, and had to stand on tiptoe to pluck the six-foot Pupasse's dress to gain her attention.

And they did help her generously. A new sheet of fool's-cap was procured, and torn in two, lengthwise, and pinned in a long strip. One by one, each little girl took it, and, retiring as far as possible, would put her hand into her pocket, and, extracting her list, would copy it in full on the new paper. Then she would fold it down, and give it to the next one, until all had written.

"Here, Pupasse; here are all our sins. We give them to you; you can have them."

Pupasse was radiant; she was more than delighted, and the more she read the better pleased she was. Such a handsome long list, and so many sins she had never thought of— never dreamed of! She set herself with zeal to commit them to memory. But a hand on the door — Madame Joubert! You never could have told that those little girls had not been sitting during the whole time, with their hands clasped and eyes cast up to the ceiling, or moving their lips as the prayer-beads glided through their fingers. Their versatility was really marvelous.

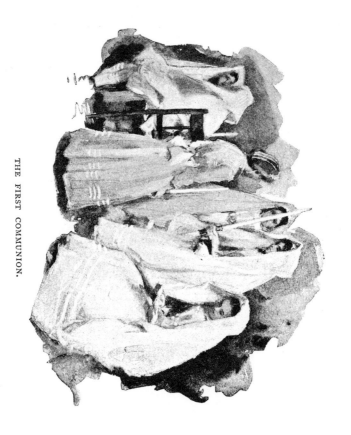

THE FIRST COMUNION.

Poor Pupasse! God solved the dilemma of her education, and madame's increasing sensitiveness about her appearance in the fifth class, by the death of the old grandmother. She went home to the funeral, and never returned—or at least she returned, but only for madame. There was a little scene in the parlor: Pupasse, all dressed in black, with her bag of primary books in her hand, ready and eager to get back to her classes and fools' caps; madame, hesitating between her interests and her fear of ridicule; Madame Joubert, between her loyalty to school and her conscience. Pupasse the only one free and untrammeled, simple and direct.

That little school parlor had been the stage for so many scenes! Madame Joubert detested acting—the comedy, as she called it. There was nothing she punished with more pleasure up in her room. And yet—

"Pupasse, *ma fille*, give me your grammar."

The old battered, primitive book was gotten out of the bag, the string still tied between the leaves for convenience in hanging around the neck.

"Your last punishment: the rule for irregular verbs. Commence!"

16

"I know it, Madame Joubert; I know it perfectly, I assure you."

"Commence!"

"Irregular verbs—but I assure you I know it—I know it by heart—"

"Commence, *ma fille!*"

"Irregular verbs—irregular verbs—I know it, Madame Joubert — one moment—" and she shook her right hand, as girls do to get inspiration, they say. "Irregular verbs— give me one word, Madame Joubert; only one word!"

"That—"

"Irregular verbs, that—irregular verbs, that—"

"See here, Pupasse; you do not know that lesson any more than a cat does"—Madame Joubert's favorite comparison.

"Yes, I do, Madame Joubert! Yes, I do!"

"Silence!"

"But, Madame Joubert—"

"Will you be silent!"

"Yes, Madame Joubert; only—"

"Pupasse, one more word—and—" Madame Joubert was forgetting her comedy— "Listen, Pupasse, and obey! You go home and learn that lesson. When you know it,

you can reënter your class. That is the
punishment I have thought of to correct
your 'want of attention.'"

That was the way Madame Joubert put
it—"want of attention."

Pupasse looked at her—at madame, a silent but potent spectator. To be sent from
home because she did not know the rule of
the irregular verbs! To be sent from home,
family, friends!—for that was the way Pupasse put it. She had been in that school—
it may only be whispered—fifteen years.
Madame Joubert knew it; so did madame,
although they accounted for only four or five
years in each class. That school was her
home; Madame Joubert — God help her!—
her mother; madame, her divinity; fools'
caps and turned-up skirts, her life. The old
grandmother—she it was who had done
everything for her (a *ci-devant* rag-picker,
they say); she it was who was nothing to
her.

Madame must have felt something of it
besides the loss of the handsome salary for
years from the little old withered woman.
But conventionality is inexorable; and the
St. Denis's great recommendation was its

conventionality. Madame Joubert must have felt something of it,—she must have felt something of it,—for why should she volunteer? Certainly madame could not have imposed *that* upon *her*. *It must* have been an inspiration of the moment, or a movement, a *tressaillement*, of the heart.

"Listen, Pupasse, my child. Go home, study your lesson well. I shall come every evening myself and hear it; and as soon as you know it, I shall fetch you back myself. You know I always keep my word."

Keep her word! That she did. Could the inanimate past testify, what a fluttering of fools' caps in that parlor — "Daily Bees," and "Weekly Couriers," by the year-full!

What could Pupasse say or do? It settled the question, as Madame Joubert assured madame, when the tall, thin black figure with the bag of books disappeared through the gate.

Madame Joubert was never known to break her word; that is all one knows about her part of the bargain.

One day, not three years ago, ringing a bell to inquire for a servant, a familiar murmuring fell upon the ear, and an old abécédaire's eyes could not resist the temptation to look through the shutters. There sat Pupasse; there was her old grammar; there were both fingers stopping her ears—as all studious girls do, or used to do; and there sounded the old words composing the rule for irregular verbs.

And you all remember how long it is since we wore funnel-shaped hoop-skirts!